D0324434

"Hud," she said, a lit
understanding dawne

"Yeah?"

"You like women. A lot of women."

"You're going to hold it against me that I like women?"

He was just a breath away from reminding her that her precious Chuck apparently liked women, too, and by the way, Hud had never cheated on *anyone*. But he couldn't do It. He couldn't hurt her by throwing that in her face.

"No," she said, shaking her head, still obviously drunk and confused. "It's just...just..."

Now he hated himself for bringing this up at all. It wasn't the time or place. She couldn't make good decisions. He was an idiot.

"Never mind. Forget I said anything."

"Don't be mad," she said softly, reaching for his arm. "Please."

"I'm not mad."

"Promise?" she said, wiping at her cheeks.

To make his point, he pulled her into his arms. She snuggled into his chest, as she always did, and he squeezed tighter, as he always did. She snuggled to get comfort, and he squeezed to keep her in his arms.

It just never worked.

WELCOME TO WILDFIRE RIDGE!

Dear Reader,

Welcome to the third book in the Wildfire Ridge miniseries. Some of you may recognize our heroine, Joanne, from an earlier book, *Airman to the Rescue*. The moment my editor said, "Poor Joanne," about her character in *Airman*, I knew I would give her a happily-ever-after of her own...someday. Fast-forward three books later in this world, and I finally get to tell you the story of this incredibly strong single mother who's raising her son and running a bridal boutique. Does she sound like supermom? Okay, I get why you might think that, but she's far from perfect. And since blowing up her life at the age of sixteen, Joanne has rarely taken chances and has played it safe. Especially when it comes to love.

Enter Lieutenant Hudson "Hud" Decker. With a series name like Wildfire Ridge, you knew I'd have a firefighter hero, right? Hud and Joanne come with a bit of a combustible history. When their young first love burned out (I can't seem to stop with the fire metaphors), they managed to salvage their friendship. But when Joanne is jilted at the altar, Hud isn't going to just put her back together for someone else this time. Ironically, playboy Hud has never quite gotten over his first love and this may be just the right moment for a second chance. First, he'll have to convince Joanne he's worth taking the risk for a chance at forever this time, and it won't be easy.

I hope you enjoy.

Heatherly Bell

The Right Moment

———

Heatherly Bell

HARLEQUIN

SPECIAL
EDITION

HARLEQUIN®
SPECIAL
EDITION™

Recycling programs
for this product may
not exist in your area.

ISBN-13: 978-1-335-89445-8

The Right Moment

Copyright © 2020 by Heatherly Bell

This edition published by arrangement with Harlequin Books S.A.

For questions and comments about the quality of this book,
please contact us at CustomerService@Harlequin.com.

Harlequin Enterprises ULC
22 Adelaide St. West, 40th Floor
Toronto, Ontario M5H 4E3, Canada
www.Harlequin.com

Printed in U.S.A.

Heatherly Bell tackled her first book in 2004 and now the characters that occupy her mind refuse to leave until she writes them a book. She loves all music but confines singing to the shower these days. Heatherly lives in Northern California with her family, including two beagles—one who can say hello and the other a princess who can feel a pea through several pillows.

To the real Iris and K.R.

Chapter One

Her groom was late.

Joanne Brant peeked through the bridal tent the wedding coordinators had set up outdoors. From here, she'd walk with her best friend Hudson Decker down a rose-petal-covered path to the glass-enclosed gazebo in the middle of a meadow. Every touch, from her Vera Wang dress to the gardenia garlands decorating the outside of the gazebo to the string quartet now tuning was breathtaking. Beautiful.

Still no sign of Chuck.

She was nervous enough as it was. Where was he? They were supposed to get started soon. She worried a manicured fingernail between her teeth.

This didn't make sense. Chuck was always punctual, sometimes to a fault. Stomach churning, she wondered what could be the cause of the delay. Was he hurt? Caught in traffic? Accident?

It had better be a good excuse.

"What time is it?" Joanne asked Nora Higgins, her maid of honor and head seamstress at Joanne's bridal boutique. "I don't have my cell phone with me."

"Um." Nora glanced at hers. "It's one thirty."

"What? *One thirty*? He's half an hour late. How did I not realize that? We're half an hour late to start!"

This wasn't funny. When he finally showed up, she'd... She'd... Well, she'd marry him.

"I'm sure he's got a good reason," said Monique Brandt, Joanne's cousin, and another bridesmaid.

"Maybe traffic is bad." Eve Wiggins, Joanne's IT person, always went with logic.

But Chuck always accounted for traffic because he hated to speed even more than he hated to be late.

Hudson or "Hud," her best friend and the one who'd give her away in place of her late father, strode into the tent. He was six foot plus of hard body, and every time he walked into the bridal tent every one of her bridesmaids licked lips and tossed hair.

"What's happening?" His tone was clipped. Annoyed. It was no secret that he was not a fan of Chuck Ellis.

Right now, neither was Joanne. If he embarrassed

her by being much later, she might go on their honeymoon to the Bahamas alone. That would teach him.

"I need my cell phone," she said to anyone who would listen. "Where is it?"

"Yeah, maybe he's been texting you," Nora said.

"He should not be texting you," Hud said. "He should have his ass here. Now. That's what he should be doing."

"Maybe there's a problem, though," Joanne said, as always, making excuses for Chuck.

Emily Parker-McAllister, the event planner who ran weddings at Fortune Valley Family Ranch, walked in, a practiced smile on her face. "Looks like we're missing a groom. Do we need to delay much longer?"

"I'll check," Joanne said. "Who has my cell phone?"

It took far too many minutes to find her phone, set to vibrate and hidden under three different garment bags. She glanced down at it. Her phone had blown up with text messages from Chuck.

I'm sorry.

I can't do this.

Are you going to answer me?

I know I should have said something sooner.

And the last most devastating message of all:

I'm not coming.

Joanne dropped her phone and slumped on the closest chair, nearly falling over. She felt as if all the color had drained out of her face. This wasn't happening. It couldn't be. Not to her. After so much planning. The perfect dress. Perfect venue. She owned a bridal boutique. She was supposed to know weddings.

This didn't make any sense. Chuck had meant safety and security to Joanne for the past year. They were well suited to each other in many ways. Compatible. Chuck had claimed to want children with Joanne and was already saving for their future education.

He was reliable. Steady.

He'd made her feel secure and wanted never even once looking at another woman. This was so out of character for him. What could have possibly changed his mind?

"Is he hurt?" Nora said. "Has there been an accident?"

"What's wrong?" Hud demanded.

Oh, God. Too many questions. She couldn't speak. It seemed as though Hud's words were coming through a voice changer in slow motion. Her bridesmaids, eyes wide, jaws gaping, looked like caricatures of themselves. They knew something was horribly wrong. Maybe Joanne hadn't been the best person in the world during her thirty-two years on earth, but even she didn't deserve this. No one did. Unbearable humiliation and shame tore through her.

When she still hadn't answered anyone, Hud crouched low in front of her, right in her line of vision. His eyebrows were drawn together in confusion, or concern. "Jo…tell me."

"He's not hurt but…" She met Hud's green gaze, so kind, so worried. "He's…he's not coming."

Both Monique and Nora gasped.

"I'll be right back," Emily said, and left them.

"What do you *mean* he's not coming?" Hud asked.

Her best friend was the only one in the room who still didn't get it. When Joanne didn't elaborate, Hud searched for her phone and picked it up off the floor. Reading the messages, he then cursed loudly enough to make Eve, Monique and Nora move closer to Joanne and circle her, putting shaking hands on her shoulders. But Joanne wondered why *she* wasn't crying. Why she wasn't devastated. She simply felt… humiliated.

And in all honesty, a tiny bit numb. Make that more than a tiny bit. Shock, she assumed.

She'd had doubts too, these last two weeks, but those were normal. Right? They were called wedding day jitters for a reason. *Am I making a mistake? Do I really love him?*

All normal.

Joanne had told herself that the tiny spark between them would grow with more time. The important thing to her was that she had a fiancé with a rock steady plan for their future. And he was committed to her. Ha! What a joke.

"Where is he?" Hud said in a low menacing voice. "I'll go get him for you."

He would, too. If she'd wanted him to, Hud would find Chuck, hog-tie him and drag him to the ceremony. He'd proceed to threaten him to within an inch of his life if he tried to run again.

"You can't. He…doesn't want to…get married." The words came out slow and measured, as if she were trying them on for size. She was almost too shaken to speak.

"Then he shouldn't have asked you."

But Hud didn't know that she'd been the one to suggest marriage in the first place. She wanted to settle down. Her sixteen-year-old son, Hunter, nearly grown now, it was finally time for her life to begin. She wanted a life partner and didn't want to be alone anymore. She'd waited so long and sacrificed so much. Worked long hours putting herself through fashion design school while raising a child. She'd opened a successful bridal shop with seed money from her father and put in long hours.

Chuck had agreed that marriage was a good idea, too, and claimed he was ready. He'd given her the ring, handed it to her over breakfast one morning, certain she'd accept it since the whole thing had been her idea. There was never an actual proposal, almost a business agreement.

One he'd backed out of at the last minute.

Outside, a small commotion had started. Confused and annoyed voices. "I gave up a golf date for this," someone said. "Do we get the presents back? Because I'm not bringing another one if they try this again!"

She heard her son's voice, or was that his father's? They sounded so similar. Her mother would be heartbroken when she heard the news. She'd liked Chuck. Thought he was good for Joanne. Bad enough Dad had passed away before he could see Joanne married, but now this. Mom didn't take humiliation any better than Joanne did.

Emily walked inside the tent. "Everything's taken care of. We're letting everyone know that a small emergency has prevented the wedding from going through today. People are beginning to leave now. Your family will probably want to talk to you."

Yes. Her mother. *Hunter.* Oh God, she'd have to explain this to her son. She already embarrassed him enough just by breathing.

"I'm going to find Aunt Ramona and explain," Monique said, rubbing Joanne's shoulder. "Calm her down."

"Please," Joanne said, then turned to Emily. "I'm so sorry about this. Thank you for everything."

"We'll talk again soon." Emily excused herself.

And there would be plenty to talk about. Such as food for the reception that might rot before it could be consumed. A DJ who would insist on being paid regardless. The minister. A deposit they'd never get back.

Hud stopped pacing in front of Joanne. "What do you want me to do? I'll do anything."

"Get me out of here. I can't talk to anyone right now. Please…just take me home."

Like her groom, the tears didn't show up. Not later that day, nor later that night.

Hud had driven her home, she'd changed from her beautiful sweetheart collar Valentino dress—being the owner of a bridal boutique had its perks—and dropped on the bed wearing nothing but her underwear. Laying back, she laced hands behind her neck. She needed time to think. To be with her own private thoughts. She'd asked Hud to leave, but in his typical maddening style, he'd refused.

She could hear him downstairs, doing something in the kitchen, opening the door to someone. Talking to them while she lay in her bed staring up at the ceiling wondering why she'd ever thought marrying Chuck would be a good idea.

Had she really been that desperate to finally get

married? For another child? For a true partner, both in bed and in life?

She's upstairs. Yeah, I'll have her call you. Thanks for bringing all the food. Sure, we'll eat it all. Don't worry.

Then presumably on his phone:

Bastard...just need two minutes alone...no, I'm just kidding...sort of.

Joanne groaned. Sounded as though Emily might have brought the food from the reception so that at least it wouldn't completely go to waste. Great. Wonder if between all of her friends and family she could get rid of all the meat, scalloped potatoes, rolls and vegetables?

Later, she wasn't sure how much later, but the bedroom had darkened and long shadows filtered through her blinds. She'd just changed into shorts and a tee and sat back down on the bed with a pad of paper when Hud again opened her bedroom door.

"Jo."

She didn't answer and kept her back to him. Let him go away and leave her be. He was beginning to piss her off. She had a life to reconsider and re-plan in case anyone cared.

"Joanne," he commanded.

"Go away."

He knelt beside her bed and handed her something. Something cold, metallic and small. It seemed to be a phone.

"You need to answer Hunter's texts. He's at Matt's and freaked out. They both need to know exactly what happened."

Oh God. Hunter. He'd been scheduled to stay with his father, Matt, and his new wife, Sarah, at their home for a month this semester. The idea was to give her and Chuck time to adjust to married life after their honeymoon. Hunter had to be wondering what was going on. And Mom. It was a shock she wasn't at the front door banging it down. She assumed she had Monique to thank for that.

"And your mother," Hud continued. "If you don't call or text her, she's coming right over."

No. She didn't want Mom coming over now. She just wanted to be left alone, not that Hud would listen.

Hud stood in the doorway waiting, arms crossed over his wide chest, watching her carefully from under hooded eyes.

What was she supposed to tell her son? She was too ashamed to come out with the harsh truth. *I'm sorry. Chuck was a loser. But instead of me realizing that in time, I let him fool me. He simply told me what I wanted to hear. And I was too desperate to believe it.* Hunter didn't need to know all the details because he was still technically a child. A man child, her son, with dreams of becoming a Marine. Maybe she could text him, his preferred mode of communication, and she didn't have to *sound* upbeat. She just had to write happy and inspirational words. She'd never wanted to be a Hallmark card writer as badly as she did at this moment.

Hey, honey. Something happened to Chuck and he couldn't make it to the wedding so we canceled. Don't worry, everything is going to be okay.

Hunter: What? He's dead?

Joanne: No! All is okay. We'll talk soon. Have fun with your Dad.

Hunter: Still getting married later?

How was she supposed to answer that question? There was no point to lying. She told herself that he'd know sooner or later. All they'd need to do was mention it to one person in Fortune, where it would spread like their wildfires.

Joanne: I don't know. Maybe not. I need to think.

Hunter: You going to the Bahamas?

It hadn't even occurred to her to go. In the Bahamas she wouldn't know what to do by herself for two weeks. Granted, she'd be in a luxurious honeymoon suite, but still. She could hide out in the Bahamas or here. She chose her comfortable and familiar bed.

But what if she told everyone she was going to the Bahamas? They'd at least leave her alone for a while.

Joanne: You know what? Maybe I should!

Hunter: You should. I say go for it!

She finished texting with Hunter, with further assurances that if she went to the Bahamas (she was not) she'd have loads of fun. She'd surf (in her dreams), snorkel (please), and take plenty of selfies.

She glared at Hud. "Okay. Done. Happy?"

Exhausted by the effort, she threw the phone down. Hud gave her a "nice try" look and reminded her, "Your mother. Now."

"Really?"

"Monique told her everything but she wants to hear it from you." He glanced at his wristwatch. "And you have about ten minutes to do it or she'll be here. With food. And you have enough food downstairs to open up a restaurant."

"I need to think. Figure out what my next steps are. Hud, I'm the owner of a bridal boutique who just got jilted! Do I look like a person who can make a phone call right now?"

"You do."

"Damn it!" He wasn't going to let this go. Joanne

picked up her phone and dialed, steeling herself for the onslaught.

"Joanne! Oh, my darling. I'm sososo sorry," her mother started in on the waterworks without delay. "Chuck didn't show! You of all people don't deserve this."

"I'm okay."

"Of course you're not okay. Don't hide the pain, dear. Just deal with it, work through it. There are no shortcuts. You'll be better for it. What stage are you in?"

Joanne wrinkled her nose. "Stage?"

"Grief. There are seven stages of grief and you should be at stage one right now. Though I know you've always been such an overachiever. But don't rush it, honey."

Joanne wondered if stage one was anger because right now she could feel it bubbling up inside her.

Chuck was nothing but an ass who didn't have enough courage to face her. If he'd changed his mind, he could have told her before today.

But her mother always brought everything down to a self-improvement book to read, or a supplement to take. Perhaps a vitamin. Meditation. She wanted to help, but Joanne didn't think life was ever that simple. All the plans she'd had were gone. Plus, she was the owner of the only bridal shop in town and she'd been stood up at the altar.

Was there a supplement for that?

"I'll be right over with some of my chicken soup. Hud says you have too much food there now as it is, but nothing is better for a broken heart than my chicken soup. Remember I fed you this soup after you and Hud broke up? After Dad died? You know it's got my special ingredient. Love."

"That sounds…wonderful, but I'm going to be leaving for the Bahamas." Joanne cringed at the lie but if it got her mother to give her some time alone there was no harm done.

"Alone?" she screeched. "Honey, no! You'll just get depressed."

"Um, no, no. Not alone. I'm going with…with Hud."

Hud, who had been listening in the doorway quirked a brow, then slowly shut the door to her bedroom.

"You and Hud? That sounds like a wonderful idea. No one cheers you up like he can. He's absolutely the best medicine next to my chicken soup. Plus you'll be the envy of every woman who thinks you two are actually together."

Ha! Her and Hud together. No, that had happened many years ago and they'd been lucky simply to salvage their friendship from the disaster.

She wouldn't ever do anything to mess with that.

Chapter Two

Hud Decker had a choice.

Find Chuck Ellis, kill him and hide the body. It could be done. He had friends. Friends who owed him.

But who was he kidding? As the lieutenant running Firehouse 57, a murder charge wouldn't look so hot on the résumé. No. "Chuck E." wasn't worth it. He didn't deserve Joanne, never had, never would, and might have actually come to that realization himself. Good for him, then. Unfortunately, his timing couldn't have been worse. He'd embarrassed Jo in front of family and friends, which made Hud want to destroy him. But he couldn't. Wouldn't. Instead, he'd put Jo back together. Maybe, when she finished writing all her lists and making new plans, she'd realize this was all for the best. They'd laugh about idiot Chuck breaking up via text message like the coward that he was.

I would have shown up. She should have been mine.

No, that wasn't right. He didn't deserve her, either. Not after the damage he'd caused. He'd been lucky to enjoy her close friendship and had learned to accept over the years that it had to be enough.

Hud was still dressed in his tux, but had removed the jacket and cummerbund, rolled up the sleeves and lost the tie. When Emily and her entourage arrived with the platters upon platters of food, they'd stuffed everything they could into plastic bowls and into the refrigerator. The rest they'd arranged on the counters, on the kitchen table, dining table and even the family room. He'd never seen so much food in one place in his life and he worked in a firehouse with men who often ate like it was their last meal. Emily had suggested giving some to family and friends. Before she left, he offered her a platter.

He'd take food over to the station right now, only he didn't want to leave Jo until Nora and Eve arrived. They'd texted him that they were on their way. Apparently, Monique was already trying to book an earlier flight back to Colorado. He also had to get home to change out of his suit and pick up Rachel,

the dog he'd adopted from Paws n Pilots, a local rescue. Jo had wanted him to name her Coco, and Hud
had called her the ridiculous name for about a day.
Then he put his foot down. If he were going to provide a home for a cockapoo mix who was more poo-
dle than cocker, *he'd* get to name her. End of story.
And yes, he'd named her Rachel after his first celeb-
rity crush, the character from the TV show *Friends*.

And if he was going to stay here much longer, he'd
need to get Rachel. If he left her alone for too long,
his furniture would pay dearly.

Needing something to do while he waited, he
packed up the food, using Tupperware and alumi-
num foil. He began to assign them. Three platters for
the fire station, one for the police station. One he'd
send up to Wildfire Ridge Outdoor Adventures, one
to Pimp Your Pet and another to Magnum Aviation.

Next, he called up friends and asked whether
they had dinner plans. First come, first served. They
started arriving an hour later, while Joanne continued to stay in her room. The last time he'd looked in
on her she'd dressed in shorts and a tank and was sitting on top of the covers probably writing one of her
lists. She loved her lists. Her order. He hoped "kill
Chuck and ask Hud to hide the body" was at the top
of this new list. That made sense to him.

What didn't make any sense was the weird tinge
of relief that had washed through him the moment
he realized that Chuck wasn't showing. The wedding

wouldn't happen. Guilt pulsed through him, making his gut burn. This was not something he should celebrate. He should be a better friend to Jo even if he'd never been one of Chuck's fans.

No, that had been Jo's mother and most of her girlfriends. They saw a man who billed himself as someone ready to commit, settle down, have a family. The women ate it up. Most of all Jo.

Hud told himself that what Chuck had done didn't have anything to do with him. Jo listened to him, but in the end, she made her own decisions. Like Chuck. And if Chuck was weak enough to allow Hud's dislike of him to play a role in all this, then he was even less of a man than Hud had realized.

If it had been him, he wouldn't have let an old boyfriend stop him from marrying Jo. Nothing could have stopped him.

Jett from Magnum Aviation and his wife showed up first. They were on a tight budget and were happy to take some of the food off his hands.

Hud called his good friend Ty Brody from the station and asked him to come pick up food for the guys. Together they loaded boxes of food into the backseat of his truck.

"Sorry about what happened."

By now, it would be all over their small town. *No wedding. Did you hear? The groom didn't show.*

"Jackass," both Hud and Ty said at once.

"And Jo? How's she doing?" Ty asked.

"I don't know. She's making a list."

"If the guy can't hack the pressures of wedding day, he'd run at the slightest hint of trouble. She's better off."

"Yeah. Try telling her that."

"This wasn't the way to do it, agreed. Hate to say it, though, but this could be your moment."

"For *what*?"

"You and Jo, together again."

"Ancient history."

Ty grinned and waggled his eyebrows. "Then how about a reboot?"

"She's probably going to hate all men for a while."

"Aw, crap. Probably right."

It wasn't that Hud hadn't ever pictured the 2.0 version. He couldn't even blame his mistakes on youth or an imperfect understanding of relationships. Because even back then, he'd somehow…just known.

And still blown it all to hell.

He'd had all the arrogance and conceit of a kid who'd just discovered the wonders of sex. It had made sense for them to see other people and he'd suggested that. Who met their soulmate at sixteen?

He'd tried to recover, tried to get her back, but by then it was too late. Their lives were changed by one careless impulse and placed on a trajectory that would keep them apart for years.

Hud handed Ty the keys to his house. "Bring me

Rachel, her food and a change of clothes? I'm staying until her girlfriends come by."

"What about her mom?" Ty asked. "Can't she come over?"

"Jo told her mom she was going on the honeymoon anyway. With me."

"Dude! Don't you wish."

"Think she wants some time alone before everyone starts pitying her. I mean, I get it."

"She knows *you* won't feel sorry for her." Ty nodded.

True enough. Hud would never feel sorry for Jo, though he did feel compassion for what she'd been through. But he'd always been tough on himself, his staff, family, friends, and of course, Jo. He saw no point in regretting what could not be changed. Time to toughen up. She'd have to get over this jerk and the sooner the better. He'd make it happen. Hud would make sure she didn't spend any more time on the loser than he was worth.

Maybe she'd come to understand on her own that being with Chuck in the first place had been a mistake. Deciding to marry him? Pure insanity. Hud didn't believe a lifetime commitment could be based purely on being practical and passing some kind of compatibility test the way Jo claimed she and Chuck had done. There had to be passion and connection, too. He hadn't seen a spark between them but then again maybe he wasn't the most impartial judge.

But he'd once accused Jo of not being in-love with Chuck. She'd protested. A little too harshly. Almost like she was trying to convince herself.

After Ty took off, Hud went inside and checked the time. Joanne would need to eat, so he heated some canned soup instead of the leftovers he didn't think she was ready to see and brought it upstairs with a glass of the sweet tea she loved.

She was still writing the damn list. She looked up when he came in. "What now?"

"Time to eat something." He set the bowl of soup on her nightstand.

"Okay," she said, and put the notepad down. "Ugh. You're such a pain."

"You know this. Why be surprised by it now?"

"I don't know why you don't just go home and let me be."

"Because you have to eat." He sat on the edge of her bed, forcing her to move.

She did, and her top shifted to reveal one smooth bare shoulder. One *shoulder*, in a bed, and he was already fantasizing.

Do not. Go. There.

"What do you have?" She sat up straighter.

"Soup." He reached for the bowl, offering it to her. "I'll force-feed you if I have to."

"In your dreams, buddy." She squinted at him, showing a little bit of the sass he loved.

"Don't make me."

She took the bowl. "Did my mother really come over here anyway?"

"Nope. This is canned and from your cupboard."

"What? No special ingredients?"

"Piss and vinegar."

"Ew, and you expect me to *eat* this?"

She took a spoonful. He was sure it was because she realized that he wasn't moving or going anywhere until she ate.

"Why did he do this to me?"

"Because he's an ass."

"No, I mean, really. Why not just tell me before the wedding day and save me some trouble? Not to mention the shame. Even if I've been through a lot worse than this, it's just not okay. You know I can't stand for people to pity me and that's what they're all doing."

He winced because he was somewhat involved in the "worse than this." "Not me." He nudged his chin to indicate she should take another spoonful.

Jo wrongly believed that when people pitied her, it meant somehow she was pitiful. Not true, but she had a little misfire in her brain where it came to this. In his mind, she deserved some sympathy and should accept that nobody was cruel enough not to feel sorry for what she'd been through.

"Of course, not you, but everyone else." She had another bite or two of soup, stared off into space and dropped the spoon. "What do I do? How do I get past this and save my business?"

His chest pinched uncomfortably and he glanced at the notepad which did indeed have a numbered list. "What does the list say?"

She nudged her chin at the list. "Go ahead. You know you want to."

He picked it up and read:

1. Figure out if I can return the wedding dress or look into other ways of selling it.
2. How much do I still owe on the dinner? Check statements.
3. Make a list of all expenses and demand he reimburse me.
4. Get back to work immediately so everyone sees that this won't affect the business.
5. Call Mom.
6. Assess any other damage control.

The list went on, but Hud stopped reading there.

"I don't see 'ask Hud to help me get rid of Chuck and hide the body.' I'll do it. You know I will." He tried a smile.

"I know." She sighed and finished the rest of the soup, somehow, then handed it back to him and went back to her list. "Will you leave me alone?"

"For now. But Nora and Eve are on their way." He shut the door against her groan.

A few minutes later, Ty was at the door with a change of clothes for Hud, and Rachel at the end of a leash. In typical fashion, her butt wiggled at Mach speed, and she tried her best to climb him like a tree. She wore her pearl studded pink collar that Jo had insisted he buy from the *Pimp Your Pet store*.

He picked Her Highness up, waited for her to lick and slobber him, then carried her upstairs. "You've got a job to do, Rachel, and the last thing I need is any shit from you. It's been a bad day."

One thing he'd realized about Rachel early on: she should have been a therapy dog. At the station, she'd wrapped everyone around her paw in a couple of minutes. Even the old-timers, who swore they'd never own a "froufrou" dog like her. Once he'd been one of them. But Rachel was a good dog. She was smart and already knew how to roll over and play dead. Until he gave her the go-ahead she wouldn't move from her spot. It was uncanny.

"Someone's here to see you." Hud set Rachel down at the edge of the bed, where she instinctively sensed the need to be closer. She belly crawled to Jo until she was just inches from her face. She licked her nose.

"Oh, Coco," Jo said, because she was his biggest pain in the ass.

"Rachel," he ground out.

He shut the door, hoping Rachel would do her thing.

* * *

Cleaning always helped with thinking. That's how Joanne found herself on her hands and knees an hour later, scrubbing the kitchen floor tile. Coco sat nearby head cocked in mild interest.

"Don't give me that look, it's cheaper than therapy."

Hud had left Coco with her and gone off to take care of something on Wildfire Ridge, where he occasionally picked up a guide shift on his days off. He wouldn't be back until tomorrow.

Joanne scrubbed, putting her back into it. She pictured erasing Chuck out of her life. He'd stepped on this floor and gotten it dirty, the bastard. First, she imagined erasing his eyes. Then his nose. Lips and jawline next. Finally, when only his stupid chin was left, she wiped it away furiously.

She'd always hated his pointy chin.

The doorbell rang and Coco barked as if to announce danger was clearly looming on the other side.

"Calm down."

Joanne carried Coco into her bedroom, set her down and assured her all was well, then went to open the front door. She'd already been warned by Hud that Nora and Eve were on their way. That was good. They could discuss plans for the boutique. For a while now, she'd wanted Eve to make one of those pixel thingies for the boutique's Facebook page. Then start some ads. Maybe she should expand.

Well, not now that she had wedding bills to pay.
But soon. The Taylor wedding was coming up and
Joanne had worked hard to get their business. The
wedding of the year in Fortune, and Joanne had sold
four of her designs to them. Some of her best work.
All that remained was for them to choose one final
design and she and Nora would order the material
and start sewing.

So, at least her professional life was intact, even
if it had to be weird for the brides who had heard
about her wedding day fail. Still, she'd recover from
all this. She had to.

When Joanne opened the front door, Nora grabbed
her in a hug. "Oh, Joanne."

Ugh. "I'm okay. Really."

"How can you be?"

"It's a break-up. I've been through them before."

"But this is different." Eve said, walking inside.
"I brought cookies. Your favorite."

"You shouldn't have. I have a ton of food here, including desserts. Someone has to eat it." There had
to be twenty or more bottles of champagne, not to
mention the wedding cake.

The. Wedding. Cake.

She'd almost forgotten.

Her friends followed Joanne into the kitchen.

Opening up the refrigerator, she found dozens
of containers of food crowding every shelf. Hud's
doing. He was an organizer, a leader and someone

who always took charge. The three-tier cake had been boxed, labeled "cake" and placed in the refrigerator, which was exploding with plastic-wrapped platters of food.

"And Hud already gave a lot of this away." Joanne reached for a box. "Cake, anyone?"

Both Eve and Nora glanced at each other.

Nora shrugged. "Well, it would be crazy to turn cake down."

"And I'm not crazy," Eve said.

"I have to agree. We're very sane women here." Joanne sliced into the top layer with joy, tossing aside the plastic couple where they landed on the clean floor. That was the end of the plastic faux Joanne and Chuck Ellis. "I wasn't hungry earlier, but now I'm famished."

Two hours or so later, the cake was in pieces. Literally. Taking zero care to appearance, each one of them had used their own fork to cut into the cake any which way. Taking what they wanted in haphazard patterns. Leaving the rest.

"Who knew a cake could look so ugly?" Nora said.

"We went after it pretty hard." Joanne licked her fork.

Eve cleared her throat. "Joanne, we have to talk about it. *You* have to talk about it."

"She's right," Nora said. "Chuck left you. Aren't you even going to find out why?"

Joanne had considered it, to be fair. During all the hours today that she'd stared at the ceiling and worked on her lists of what to do next. She'd wondered. Should she ask him if she'd done anything wrong? Pushed too hard? Nagged too much about all his away baseball games?

But, no. Far from it. She'd encouraged him to pursue his dreams. Admired him, even, for never giving up on someday reaching the majors. All the time Chuck spent traveling meant that her life hadn't really changed all that much. The difference being that after marriage, he'd move in with her, and they'd start a family. He would give her more children. At thirty-two, some days it felt like she was running out of time.

She'd done nothing wrong, unless you wanted to count the decision to agree to marry him in the first place. It might have been a little...misguided.

"I don't care why," Joanne said. "No reason is good enough."

"Even I'm curious," Eve said, touching her chest. "I mean, who even does that?"

"Not a real man," Joanne said.

"A chicken shit," Nora said and they all laughed.

"I'll drink to that!" Eve said and raised a fake glass in salute.

Then Joanne remembered all of the champagne bottles in the fridge. "I can help with that!"

They drank the bubbly wine from flutes and after a while, Nora got deep. She was clearly drunk.

"You know whah I tink?"

"What?" Joanne said. She was lying on her back in the living room. All three of them were, the tops of their heads touching in a semi-circle.

"I think love is really, really...hard."

"Uh-huh," Eve said. "Preach it."

"Sooooo hard," Nora said.

"That's too bad," Eve said. "I don't think that's fair. It shouldn't be so hard."

"Guys are terrible, too. That's no help," Nora said.

"Not all guys," Joanne added.

"Word," Eve said, "Just...most. You know?"

"There are good guys. Like...um...whosit? Whatshisname?" Nora groaned. "Oh yeah. Um, lieutenant Hudson Decker."

"Yeah, but he's like...taken so you can't have him," Eve explained.

"Right." Nora nodded.

Joanne knew Nora was nodding because she felt her head bob up and down against hers. "Wait. Who has him?"

Two heads bobbed up and were right in Joanne's line of vision. She actually blinked it was so sudden.

"You," Nora said.

She shook her head. "Not me."

"Please don't tell me you haven't noticed how hot he is," Eve said, coughing. "Oh, please."

"I try hard not to notice, okay?"

It wasn't that she didn't realize Hud was the "classic" definition of handsome. That was part of the problem. Every woman noticed him, and he in turn, noticed them. Frequently.

He had sandy blonde hair, shimmering and intelligent green eyes that noticed the smallest thing, a smirk of a smile that tipped to one side when he was tired, and...well, she could go on. But again, she tried not to notice.

"That's too bad," Eve said with a deep sigh. "Because we can't date him, either. He's your ex."

"I wouldn't advise it," Joanne said. "Not unless you want to be tossed over for the latest model in a month or so."

It was one of the reasons Joanne had gravitated toward Chuck. He wasn't classically attractive and the farthest thing from a player. Not at all. But he was a coward. A liar. Not much better.

"Yeah, no thanks," Nora said. "I'm going to be thirty next year."

"I would take him," Eve said. "For one night."

"One night? That's all you want out of a man?" Joanne asked, incredulous.

"From Hud." She winked.

"Yeah," Nora said. "I bet he's good."

They both looked at her expectantly. Shocked, she sat up. "I don't know. We were teenagers!"

Eve stared, dumbfounded. "Never again, over the

years, not even once? You know when you were both lonely and between relationships. A little something-something? Never?"

"No!"

Why did everyone always ask her that?

Looks weren't everything. She had a list of qualities she wanted in a man. First and foremost was the ability to be monogamous.

And Hud had already proven himself incapable.

Chapter Three

The next day, Joanne woke up to something cold and wet on her toes. She lifted her head from the pillow to inspect.

Coco.

Oh, excuse her. *Rachel*. Which, by the way, was not a proper name for a dog, least of all a cockapoo who should clearly be named Coco. She closed her eyes again.

She'd been dreaming of warm sandy beaches. Mojitos by the pool. She wore one of the many two-piece swimsuits she'd bought for the honeymoon. A black-and-white polka-dot number that made her feel like a blonde Audrey Hepburn. The sun was toasty on her legs and her eyes were shut against the brightness of the day. Suddenly someone was pulling on her leg. Playfully. She kicked, hoping whoever had her foot would let go. They didn't.

"Jo," a deep and commanding male voice said.

Man, that voice. It gave her pleasant sexy shivers. Desire poured through her. She opened her eyes to check out this cabana guy or whoever was making a pass at her while she slept on the beach and found Hud staring at her. Oh. Wow. Source of sexy deep voice. A sexy man. What were the odds?

Joanne shook her head. Re-direct! Re-direct!

Hud's forehead was creased in concern.

She stretched. There were layers of cotton in her mouth. Strands of hair were stuck to her chin. She appeared to have drooled a little bit. "W-what?"

Oh, for the love of God, she was on the floor. The living room floor. She vaguely remembered eating cake and drinking champagne. No wonder she felt like death. All that sugar.

"Looks like you had some fun in here."

She followed his gaze to four empty champagne bottles and what looked like a massacred cake. It had three large knives stuck in what was left of the cake.

"Where are…?"

"I got Eve an Uber. Surprised you slept through all her moaning and apologizing."

"What about Nora?"

Hud shrugged.

"Oh yeah, she's probably already at the shop." She groaned. "What time is it?"

"Two o'clock." He gave her a hand, and she rose, swaying a little bit.

When he caught her, his large warm hand touched bare skin and it was then that she noticed…she was wearing a short T-shirt that came to her waist and cotton panties. Nothing else.

She stared at him, at her panties, then back at him. "I was hot!"

"Clearly." He bit back a smile.

"Oh, no. Coco! Is she okay?"

"I just let her outside and she peed for several minutes."

"Good girl." Joanne bent to pick up the little ball of fluff she'd come to adore and gave her a snuggle. "I'm sorry I forgot about you."

Hud was still staring at Joanne. He was staring below the waist. "Stop staring."

"Sorry," he said, raising his head to meet her gaze. "Nothing I haven't seen before."

"I need a shower." She handed Rachel back to him. "Do you mind waiting until I'm done?"

"No problem."

In the shower, she allowed the hot water to pound her aching neck. She washed her hair. Then she rinsed and applied conditioner. Used her big-toothed comb to detangle. It was her ritual and required no thinking. She appreciated that. Right now she didn't want to think about much of anything, other than maybe plan where she'd bury Chuck's body. Method of death? Poison. Anything else would require more strength than she had at the moment. Or she could beat him into a coma with her words. Pointy sharp words which would tear into his flesh and punish him for taking so much of her time.

Her money.

Her pride.

She toweled off and went for all her beauty products, neatly lined up. Moisturizing cream to hold off the wrinkles that were creeping up on her. Hair products that gave her a bouncy and glossy shine. For who? She didn't care. How about for herself? She liked to look good. Her preparations were complete when she brushed and flossed her teeth like she did every morning and evening.

Boy, it almost felt like she hadn't had a bottle of champagne and half of a chocolate cake. She felt normal.

Dressing in her yoga pants and another long T-shirt, she went downstairs to apologize to Hud for being in her underwear and on the floor when he arrived. That was embarrassing. It wasn't even her best lingerie. They were the rabbits with pink bowties cotton panties. The ones she wore on laundry day. Ugh.

From her kitchen, she saw Hud's back as he faced the yard, head lowered, hands in his pockets.

Watching Rachel as she sniffed around every bush. Crouched to pee. Then sniffed another bush. Repeat. When she finally came to him, her tail wiggling, he bent to pick her up and tenderly held her. The image of this big man holding such a tiny creature in his hands softened her heart. Hud was gentle when he wanted to be. Loving, kind and funny when he wasn't being a pain in the butt.

He stepped inside, quirking a brow when he saw her standing in front of him, arms crossed. His head bent low to allow Rachel to lick his face he looked at her from underneath his eyelashes. "What?"

"You saw me in my panties."

"So?"

"What do you mean 'so'? I want to apologize for not being dressed."

"I barely noticed. But if it bothers you that much, you want to see me naked?" He undid the top button of his cargo pants.

"Don't do it." The thought was so titillating that she covered her eyes with the heels of her hands.

"Relax. I'm not that easy. Got to buy me dinner first. Or at least a beer."

When she brought her hands down, he was giving her his easy smile. The one that reminded her how many times he'd rescued her. Cheering her up after a bad date with a guy who seemed perfect until he announced he hated "snotty nosed" kids. All the other men who were shocked that she, who seemed like such a *smart* and educated woman, had a teenage son. Didn't that mean she'd been a teenage mother? Why, yes. Yes, it did. Hud had always been there to confess that men sucked. All of them. He'd remind her that she had a wonderful son, a thriving business and great friends. At one time that had been enough. She wasn't sure how all that had changed and when she got up on her high horse and thought she needed more.

He set Rachel down. "Jo, I've got some bad news."

"Oh God, no. More?"

"I saw your mom in town. She knows I'm not in the Bahamas with you."

She faced palmed.

"It's going to be okay."

"Hud," she whispered. "I don't know where to start fixing this mess."

He opened his arms wide. "C'mere."

She went into the arms of a man who, hands down, issued the greatest hugs. He was, at heart, a big teddy bear of a man though not many realized this fact. A long time ago she'd decided that if she ever found a man who gave out hugs like Hud's, she'd marry him in a second. When that never happened, she'd settled for Chuck. But this time the hug was different, as if he was holding back. Not squeezing as tightly as normal. Probably because he felt guilty about checking her out when she was half naked. On the other hand, if that were true, why did he smell her hair?

He pulled away abruptly. "Let me get you some lunch."

"You don't have to do that."

"It's no bother. You're having sliced meat and potatoes and vegetables. You're having that forever."

"The food." She sighed. "I don't want to eat food from the devil wedding."

"Might as well eat what we can today and throw the rest away."

"What happened to all that food?" She plopped down on a stool near the counter.

Hud informed her of how many friends, family members and local community services, like a homeless shelter and another for battered women had enjoyed the food for her reception. At least it hadn't gone to waste. A few minutes later she was seated in front of a mini banquet with all the food from her almost wedding to the son of Satan. Before her were sliced meats—the best Fortune Valley Family Ranch had to offer. Marinated tri-tip, top sirloin and New York strip, freshly baked rolls from The Drip, and scalloped potatoes.

"I was supposed to eat this food as a married woman. With my husband, the son of Satan."

"You could eat it now, with your best friend, the stud." He served her a plate and plopped it in front of her. "Eat. It's actually very good. Have the last laugh on him."

"I'm worried. What's going to happen to my bridal boutique now?"

"Why should anything happen?"

She dropped her fork in emphasis. "I'm a jilted bride."

"What? It's contagious?" He smirked.

"Don't laugh. Brides can be a funny bunch. I've seen all kinds over the years. Brides who will only marry on a double-digit day, brides who will only marry on months with a full moon. I'm getting back to work, now that my mother knows the truth. Not hiding out anymore."

"Good. That's a plan."

But Joanne wondered why she still hadn't cried. Shouldn't she cry or at least want to cry?

She was more upset over the humiliation of what Chuck had put her through. Of what her brides would think. Still, she'd loved him, right? Sure, it wasn't passionate or lusty love, but it was the sort of love that grew with time. Or so she'd thought. In some countries, she and Chuck would have been matched together due to common interests and goals. They were well suited to each other.

Hud bit into a roll with a bit of hostility. "Have you talked to him yet?"

"I've had no time to talk to him."

He shrugged. "You could have texted. Emailed. Carrier pigeon. I don't know."

"I don't want to talk to him. What is there to say?"

"How about 'Hey, asswipe, you owe me money.' Click, Send." He made a motion with his fingers.

"Do you think that's all I care about? The *money*? He humiliated me."

"He humiliated himself. Too much of a coward to face you. Breaking up via text on your wedding day gives new meaning to low-down dirty coward."

She didn't disagree. But not everyone could be Hudson Decker. Not everyone would run into a burning building. Some had a built-in sense of self-preservation. Then again, Hud had built his own defenses around his heart. That heart had never been fully open to anyone. It was the one risk he wouldn't seem to take.

That aversion to emotional risk had him breaking up with her after their only time together. Little explanation. It was over. Her sixteen-year-old self had raged in hurt and confusion. In classic teenage immaturity, she'd assumed Hud was "the one." Forever. Gave him her virginity and her heart. And then he'd abandoned her.

So he'd only wanted one thing, like most boys. She'd simply retaliated by going on a date with the most popular guy at school: Matt Conner. Her only motivation had been to make Hud jealous.

She'd accomplished that, but in a much more epic

way than she'd ever planned. Matt got her pregnant their first and only time. Still, she'd gotten Hunter out of it, so no regrets. Her son had been the one bright light in her life for years.

Matt had offered to marry her, of course, but she'd turned him down. She would have a child by a boy she didn't love but that didn't mean she had to marry him. Not that she had thought Hud would want anything to do with her again, but she just couldn't go through with a marriage of convenience. She still loved Hud. Loved him all through her pregnancy, and all the intervening years since. But eventually the crazy burning young love she'd had for him as a young woman had burned itself out. It had transformed into a wonderful deep friendship that it would simply kill her to lose.

"Here we are again, Jo. I'm getting you through another breakup. This too shall pass."

"This is different. I'm done. Done with men. Done with love."

He quirked a brow. "Not you."

"Yes, me. Done, done, done, buddy." She held up her fork, making a proclamation by sweeping it in the air like a wand. "Done."

"You don't give up that easy. You own a bridal boutique, for crying out loud. Love will conquer all and all that crap."

"Not this time, Robert Frost." She made a face. "That's beautiful, by the way."

He grinned. "So I'm not a romantic. I never get any complaints."

"Have you looked in the mirror lately? Who would complain?"

"Right. Because that's me. Just another pretty face."

"Don't forget the hot bod."

He chuckled. "As long as *you* don't forget."

A moment passed between them, a microsecond in which neither one of them spoke. They simply locked gazes over her kitchen counter. The oxygen and tension lay like a coil, thick and heavy between them. It made her skin too tight and she was the first to look away.

He said something under his breath that sounded like, "chicken," but she ignored him and stood to carry her half-eaten plate of food to the sink. When she bumped elbows with him that was different, too. Instead of laughing and calling him a first-class klutz as she normally would, her stomach tightened in some kind of weird anticipation. Of what, she had no idea. But Hud didn't come through with the usual suspects, either. No jokes about how she could quit accidentally rubbing against him and admit she wanted to sleep with him again. Find out if all the rumors about his prowess in the bedroom were true.

But she'd decided long ago that she couldn't be with him again in that sense. Ever. She didn't want to add herself to his long line of women. At least she would always be able to say she'd been his first, if not his last.

"I guess I've got some calls to make."

She hadn't been looking forward to it, but when she looked, there were twenty missed calls. Not one of them from Chuck. The most recent was from poor Nora, who must have crawled out of here this morning.

Hud hung back to give her privacy, she assumed. He started throwing the rest of the food away, food she was happy to see in the trash can.

"Joanne," Nora said as she picked up the phone, obviously recognizing caller ID. "Are you as hungover as I am?"

"Worse." She whispered into the phone. "You couldn't wake me before you left? I was wearing my panties when Hud came over."

"I tried to. You said, 'if you touch me again, I'll kill you.'"

"Oh, no. I did?" She winced. "I'm sorry."

"I never knew you to be so hostile in the morning."

"What's up?" Joanne asked, getting to the point.

"Are you going to take the entire two weeks off anyway?"

"Absolutely not. I'd come in today, but you know…hangover. I'm feeling good otherwise, and I'll be in tomorrow morning first thing."

"I… I wasn't going to say anything, but if the

rumors are true, I thought you should know right away."

Joanne almost stopped Nora from telling her, because she just couldn't take any more bad news. "I should know what?"

"You've probably not been watching much sports TV lately, or ever, but apparently Chuck finally made the next round of the major leagues a few months ago. I think that's what my brother said. He keeps up with that sort of stuff."

"Really. Why wouldn't he *tell* me that?"

Getting to the majors had been Chuck's dream for years. At thirty-four, he was already old for the sport, but he wouldn't give up. His minor-league team had been on the road, but they'd never made it to the play-offs, which made September a safe month to get married.

At one time she'd admired that about him. She'd admired his assurance to know what he wanted and go after it relentlessly. In addition to that, he'd been saving for their future since early in their relationship. He'd been serious about forever.

"And...also," Nora continued, drawing her words out. "He's...um, I heard that—"

"Spit it out!"

"Okay, okay. Now, this one is just a rumor mind you, but he's got a girlfriend. Mandy Jewels, the country music singer."

"Mandy?"

Chuck didn't even like country music. Whenever Joanne had tried to get him out to the Silver Saddle in town, he'd get a migraine. But her first wild guess was that this wasn't about the music at all. He'd stuff cotton in his ears if he had to. Mandy was a beautiful girl.

And young.

"I'm so sorry. I hated to have to tell you this. Remember, it might not even be true. You know how sometimes these industry professionals try to get publicity by dating someone in the public eye."

"Don't worry about it," Joanne said, feeling her throat constrict. "I know I'm better off."

She'd have been better off with a man who had the guts to simply tell her the truth. Honesty. In such short supply when it came to the men in her life. Except for Hud, and she assumed that was simply because they had a different kind of relationship. A real and solid friendship. He wouldn't lie to her because there was no reason to anymore.

"I know you're better off," Nora said. "I didn't want to say anything, but Chuck turned out to be a jerk. A major…a major doodlehead!"

Joanne almost laughed. Almost. Unfortunately she wouldn't be laughing for the next decade. Chuck might soon have money. *Real* money. The kind of money he'd never had while he'd been with her. She didn't care about wealth, having done fine supporting her son and herself all these years. Still, the thought that he'd let her pay for this entire wedding and then not bothered to show up, or cancel in time to get their deposits back… What a dick he was.

"Is there anything else you need right now?"

She'd have thought Nora could wait to deliver this news unless she'd also called for another reason.

"Yes," she said, sounding miserable. "But I want to state right now for the record that I did everything I could."

Great. Now what? "Just tell me."

"It's Tilly Jacobs again. This time she's convinced that you being left—" Nora cleared her throat "—at the altar is bad luck for her wedding day so she wants her deposit back. The dress just needs a little tailoring. Should I give her the deposit back?"

God, no. If they gave back a deposit once she'd already sewn the dress, she'd have been out of business a long time ago. "No. Listen, I'll come down and talk to her."

"You will?"

"Can you ask her to come in and talk to me tomorrow?"

"She's actually here waiting. With her mother."

"Oh."

"I really tried, but I need your help. She wants to see for herself that you're still alive and breathing and not so devastated that you won't show your face in public."

"How ridiculous. I'll show her what a strong woman looks like."

Joanne hung up and turned to Hud. "I'm going over to the shop. Please be here when I get back."

She was for certain going to need another one of his hugs.

Chapter Four

"You look beautiful." Joanne studied Tilly's reflection in the oval-shaped mirror inside Joanne's Boutique.

She'd brought out the dress Tilly was afraid might be cursed now, had Tilly try it on, veil and all.

"I *do* look beautiful."

"See? I told you," said Tilly's long-suffering mother, Alice.

"Of course you're going to say that, *Mom*," twenty-year-old Tilly said, sounding fifteen. "But if Joanne says it, I know it must be true."

Now to set the stage.

"Picture yourself almost sashaying down the aisle,

this beautiful train following your every move like it's a part of you. You're poetry in motion. You. This beautiful dress. The veil. Like everything was made for you."

"Oh, I know what you mean." Tilly fluffed her veil. "Just like Keith was made for me. I can just picture him waiting for me at the end of the aisle. He looks so handsome in his black tux. Like a movie star. How did I get so lucky? I can't *wait* to be his wife."

There was a collective sigh from both Nora and Alice.

"Yes, yes. Of course." Joanne fought to recover. She'd lost her touch. How could she forget the groom? "This is a very special day for you and Hud—I mean, Keith!"

Wow, what was that about?

"You're right," Tilly said, turning to Joanne. "Just because you didn't get your happily-ever-after doesn't mean I won't get mine."

"Tilly!" Alice scolded. "Please."

Tilly lowered her head. "I'm sorry, Joanne."

Joanne waved a hand. "It's nothing. I'm fine now."

"Really? But if Keith left me at the altar I'd die."

"Don't be so dramatic," Alice said. "On the other hand, if Keith leaves you at the altar, your father will kill him. That isn't drama, just the facts."

Nora chuckled but Tilly glared at her mother.

"Well, you were the one who brought it up!" Alice said.

"What are you going to do about your dress? The beautiful Valentino. What a waste. Are you going to burn it?" Tilly sounded as though that were the most logical thing to do.

This gave new meaning to a "fire sale." Dang, look at her making a joke. What was *wrong* with her? And why hadn't *she* pictured Chuck at the end of the aisle, waiting?

"Don't burn it," Nora said, wringing her hands.

As if. "I won't. The dress is gorgeous. Someday it will be worn."

Nora embraced Joanne in a hug, squeezing her tight. There was genuine sympathy and compassion in the embrace, and Joanne felt it down to her marrow. Still not as good as one of Hud's. Even when he was tired.

After Tilly and her mother finally left, satisfied, Joanne headed home. As she drove, it occurred to her that she'd face many more years of working with brides, but this time with a kind of jinx over her head. She had to turn this around because she'd already lost her touch with the proper words to set the stage for the bride on her wedding day. Just didn't have it in her anymore. But surely she'd still love dressing brides after this haze finally cleared. One day, one epic fail, certainly couldn't ruin both her life *and* her business.

At home, Hud sat on the couch, arms spread out on either side watching TV, Rachel cuddled next to him on the couch. "Hey. Everything okay?"

"I need a hug," she said, sitting next to him. "On top of everything else, I think I'm going to be a pariah from now on. 'Come see the sad jilted bride, owner of the only bridal boutique in town.'"

Hud didn't say anything, just simply pulled her into a sideways hug and squeezed her tight. She closed her eyes and enjoyed the warmth of his arms as it seeped into her skin, through her clothes and straight to her bones. Straight to her heart.

"I'm still a little hung over." She pulled away. "I'm going to take a nap."

Hudson had half a mind to call the whole thing off.

He'd come up with the idea on the fly. All the guys at the station helped, because every one of them thought of Jo as their little sister, or a daughter for the old-timers. *Couldn't that idiot Chuck see that she was perfect in every way? Beautiful. Smart. A good mother. Devoted to her family.* They'd always been so impressed that he'd carried on a friendship with her all these years without ever wanting more.

It would be even better if that were true.

But what he had planned for today might backfire on him. It could make her sadder. He hoped not.

Besides, he had some apologizing to do and he did

best with actions. Even though he'd done his utmost to avert his gaze, he'd still had an eyeful of Jo's long legs leading up to that delectable heart-shaped butt.

Still, it was wrong.

Sixteen-year-olds were not known for their wisdom and maturity. Upset and angry, Hud had driven too fast and crashed his father's sweet classic Mustang when he'd heard the news that Jo was pregnant with Matt Connor's baby. He'd spent three months in the hospital in traction for a broken leg and arm. Been lucky to be alive, his parents and the doctors all said. The paramedics who had pulled him out of the car had been the reason he'd later become an EMT, then a firefighter and paramedic.

Jo had visited him in the hospital nearly every day, bringing him flowers and cards and holding his hand. Hud had still felt like a first-class idiot. Everything had happened because of his decision. Jo's future had been determined. She'd have Matt's baby and that was the end of it. She'd refused to marry Matt, and refused to marry at all. Then again, she was sixteen and would continue to live with her parents and finish school. Hud didn't even offer to marry her, knowing she'd say no. Knowing he wasn't good enough for her and probably never would be.

While Jo napped, Rachel followed him around as he filled the small rubber wading pool with water and set it in the middle of her living room. He pushed back the couch and set up chaise lounges, bringing in the heat lamps she had outside in the patio area. He hung fairy lights to give the room an atmospheric touch. Then he started the lazy island music he'd downloaded. He changed into his board shorts and started blending drinks. Mojitos. Mai tais.

When Jo came downstairs two hours later wearing her yoga pants and a T-shirt that read I Woke Up Like This, he was ready for her. Lying back on one of the chaise lounges, he held out his Mai Tai. "Join me."

She rubbed her eyes. "What…what's all this?"

"Brought the Bahamas to you." He scanned the room and all he'd done to change it into an island paradise.

She did the same and a tiny hint of a smile curved her lips and sparkled in her emerald eyes.

She wandered to the kitchen and found the blender filled with Mai Tais. "Did you make me a mojito?"

"What do you take me for? There's a pitcher in the fridge."

"This is amazing." She turned back to him, eyes wide. "You got a kiddie pool?"

"Got to have some water nearby and this is the best I could do. Belongs to a two-year-old who knows how to share. Hey, we can dip our feet in at least." He grinned. "Go put on your swimsuit. Might as well."

"I bought four of them, actually."

He took a big gulp of his drink and swallowed, worried he'd be treated to a fashion show from which he'd never recover. She sprinted up the steps with more energy than he'd seen in days.

Hud fist-pumped with Rachel, another trick he'd taught her. "I've got this."

When Jo ran back down in a red two-piece bikini that left little to the imagination, he was surprised she wasn't as self-conscious as she usually was around him. Instead, she allowed her breasts to jiggle as if she didn't realize this was even happening. He wished he could tell her to stop bouncing but he wasn't quite that noble.

"This is so thrilling!" She'd brought a towel with her that she spread on the chaise lounge. "I've always wanted to go to the Bahamas."

I'll take you. To the real place. Just say the word.

Shut up, you idiot. She just got over a very bad breakup and your assignment, which you already accepted long ago, was to put her back together. Remind her how much she's worth. Heal her heart.

For what? So she can go meet some other loser who will break her heart? No one's ever going to take care of her like I do.

True, but not the point. He rose to get her a mojito and brought it to her with a colorful straw and a parasol umbrella. She leaned back on the lounge, sunglasses on. My God, she was so adorable.

"Thank you, cabana boy," she said, accepting the drink. "Would you turn down the sun a little bit?"

Hud adjusted the heat lamp and sat back down.

"I ordered us a pizza. Take it easy with that drink because you don't have a lot in your stomach."

"Pizza delivery to the beach? Awesome."

"You'll eat, right?" He wasn't convinced.

"I'm pretty hungry." She turned to him. "No sausage?"

"Jo, I know how you take your pizza."

She sighed. "Not everyone does."

Yeah, he'd bet Chuck didn't know her favorite flower either, or how she took her coffee. He'd bet he didn't know her favorite movie was *3:10 to Yuma* or that she cried every year on the anniversary of her father's death.

Jo went through that mojito pretty fast and the pizza hadn't yet arrived. He glanced at his wristwatch. They claimed the delivery time was twenty minutes. Thirty minutes ago.

"You know what we didn't do?" Jo straightened. "Suntan lotion. We don't want to get a burn."

"Sure, why not? Let's go all in." But he rose and headed to the kitchen. "I'll make you a sandwich. Damn pizza is late."

"First, another mojito." In the kitchen, she purposely bumped into his hip as she replenished her drink, then giggled. "I'm having so much fun. This is such a great idea."

She danced to the island music as she made her way to the bathroom, presumably for the lotion. He smiled, just watching her move. She often had that effect on him.

He'd finished making the sandwich when she got back. "Eat something before you drink anymore."

"In a minute." She spread lotion on her arms. "After I finish this mojito."

"That drink is going to go right to your head. You have almost nothing in your stomach." Listen to him. Was he her father now?

She stuck her tongue out at him. "I can handle my mojitos."

"Sure." He set the plate on the floor next to her. "But eat this before Rachel does."

Rachel was already sniffing from her perch on the couch he'd pushed several feet away.

"Get my back, would you?" She handed him the lotion.

Was she kidding? "You're enjoying this game."

"I used to play make-believe with Hunter all the time. He was Batman, I was Catwoman. This is so much more fun. I haven't played like this for years."

He hadn't, either. He spread coconut-smelling lotion over Jo's back and if his hands lingered a little too long at the small of her back he could hardly be blamed. Her skin was softer than he'd remembered. Smooth and creamy. Being this close to her, touching her like this, was deeply affecting. For the first time, he gave himself permission for his desire. He didn't try to tamp it down or push it back.

She moved and abruptly stopped his momentum. "Now your back."

When her fingers lightly touched his back, rubbing in a downward motion, it could be said that he hadn't felt as turned on when women had done far more to him. And a lot farther south.

"Wow. You have a nice back. Why did I not know that?"

You haven't seen me naked since I was sixteen? Even then, it was pretty dark in the backseat of my father's car.

She continued, squeezing his lats, "Look at these doohickeys. What do you call them? Glutes and ladders? Or is that chutes and ladders?"

"Lats and traps," he said, thinking that if the pizza guy didn't show up soon, he might have to put his whole head in that kiddie pool to cool off.

Mind over matter. Mind over matter.

Any moment the doorbell would ring with the pizza delivery, or Jo would come to her senses and stop the madness. He wasn't a saint, for the love of God. To demonstrate that to both of them, he removed her hand as it was midway down his back for the fifth time.

He turned to face her. "So, the pizza…"

But she had tears in her eyes. "I'm sorry."

"What? No, don't be sorry." He was the sorry one, because he wanted to bite that plump bottom lip of hers.

"I'm trying to make myself feel better, trying to believe that someone would want me. I know, it's not fair—" Her hand covered her eyes until he brought it down.

"Wait. What?"

"You're so nice to me all the time. You did all this." She waved her hand around the room. "For me. And I'm being so unfair."

"Jo, you're drunk."

"No, I'm not!" she protested. "Is that what you think? Let me show you how un-drunk I am. If I was drunk, could I do this?"

She rose and, God help him, started toeing an imaginary line. He face-palmed. She made it halfway across the room before she slid a little, bumped into the kiddie pool and lost her footing.

"Okay, that's not fair. We both know I'm not very coordinated on a good day. Let me try again." This time she went arms out as if walking a tightrope.

"Why me?" He implored the heavens. "Stop. Come here."

She walked back to him. "Finally. Do you believe me now?"

"I believe you." Because there was a God in heaven, the doorbell rang. "The pizza."

He stood to get his wallet, and that's when Jo suddenly turned ghost white. She covered her mouth and ran for the bathroom.

"If only you'd been here sooner," he said to the kid delivering.

He set the pizza down on the counter, then went to Jo and crouched behind her, holding her hair back. It was so silky it almost slipped through his callused fingers.

"I'm such a mess," she said when she stopped and he handed her a towel. "Why don't you hate me?"

"Because I don't. No one could hate you." He held out his hand to help her stand.

"He cheated on me," she said, eyes watery. "Chuck did. With some young and beautiful girl, Mandy Jewels. The country music star."

The red-hot fire of anger coursed through his veins, quickening his pulse. He spoke through clenched teeth. *"What?"*

"And also he's now going with the major leagues."

"That's…that's really hard to believe." He meant this sincerely. He'd seen Chuck pitch.

"Really, what's wrong with me? Why are men always abandoning me?"

He would swear that his heart had stopped on a dime. That was him. He'd been the first man to leave her. Not long after Hunter was born, her father had died.

"You don't really believe that."

"Don't I? What's wrong with me?"

"Nothing, except you keep picking the wrong

men!" He seemed to be yelling a little bit. He hadn't meant to yell. Shit.

She jerked back. "You never said anything before."

"Well, you never asked."

She seemed to be considering it. "What kind of men *should* I pick? I'm a single mom. You and I both know how hard it is for me to find a decent guy. Someone who has a job and a solid future plan, someone who likes kids and wants to have some, likes pets...you know the drill."

"I have a job. I want kids. I have Rachel."

"You want kids?" Her eyes were narrowed.

"Yes!"

"Hud," she said, a little breathless as understanding dawned on her. "But you...you..."

"Yeah?"

"You like women. A lot of women."

"You're going to hold it against me that I like women?"

He was just a breath away from reminding her that Chuck apparently liked women, too, liked them young, and by the way, Hud had never cheated on *anyone*. But he couldn't do it. He couldn't hurt her by throwing that in her face.

"No," she said, shaking her head, still obviously drunk and confused. "It's just...just..."

Now he hated himself for bringing this up at all. It wasn't the time or place. She didn't have her faculties about her. She couldn't make good decisions. He was an idiot.

"Never mind. Forget I said anything."

"Don't be mad," she said softly, reaching for his arm. "Please."

"I'm not mad."

"Promise?" she said, wiping at her cheeks.

To make his point, he pulled her into his arms. She snuggled into his chest as she always did and he squeezed tighter, as he always did. She snuggled to get comfort, and he squeezed to keep her in his arms.

It just never worked.

Chapter Five

The next morning, Joanne woke up and reached for the bottled water she kept on the nightstand next to her bed. Cradling her head, she noticed she still wore her red swimsuit from last night's um… Festivities. Her incredibly revealing two-piece. She'd chosen this of all her new swimsuits to wear in front of Hud. First the panties. Now this.

"Oh no. What did I do?"

She was alone now. No Hud. Rachel was snuggled at the foot of her bed. Pieces of the evening came back to her. Hud's incredible surprise. So sweet. Oh yes, the mojitos. Too many of those. The lotion she'd spread over Hud's back, while those hard as granite muscles tensed beneath her fingertips. He was sexual desire personified. Torture. Like a dummy, she'd had too much to drink, thrown herself at him, then thrown up and headed straight into feeling sorry for herself territory without passing GO and collecting two hundred bucks.

And Hud… Oh right. He had suggested that he was the perfect man for her, or had she just imagined that? No, he had. And then they'd argued over it. Made up. Or something. She didn't remember much after that, but at some point she'd fallen asleep and vaguely recalled Hud carrying her up to bed where he'd deposited her. Alone.

Which made sense, because Hud would never have taken advantage of her in that condition. And if she hadn't been drunk, what would have happened then? For the first time in years, she was bold enough to let herself imagine it. Hud, kissing her lips, his warm tongue plundering. Taking his clothes off, then hers. Throwing her down to the bed, where he'd…

Stop it! Stop fantasizing about your best friend. This had to be the stress of being jilted at the altar and worrying about the boutique. Well, today she was back to work and showing the world that she'd moved on. Screw Chuck and the train he rode in on. She'd learned her lesson. Never count on a man to provide your happiness. A lesson she'd learned long ago but somehow forgotten. It should be okay to be alone. She'd been happy before Chuck. Dating here and there, nothing serious, but mostly focused on her business, her son, her mother and her friends.

Joanne splashed water on her face and took a look at herself in the mirror. Not great, but she'd looked worse.

Time to get on with her life.

She showered, then threw on a bathrobe and made her way downstairs, Rachel on her heels. On the kitchen counter, she found a note in Hud's writing:

Back to rotation. Dog food is on the counter
Take care of Rachel. She's depending on you.
This is your mission, and should you choose
to accept it, this note will burst into flames to
cover my tracks.
No, really. Take care of Rachel.

Joanne smiled. "Your master thinks he's funny."

She set Rachel down, and the little dog wiggled her butt and promptly peed all over her kitchen tile floor.

"Coco!"

She tilted her head as if she didn't know why, and was a little insulted that Joanne would call her by another woman's name.

"I mean, Rachel!"

Joanne opened the sliding glass door to let Rachel outside in her enclosed backyard. She cleaned up the mess, then found Rachel's food bowl and poured a cup of the dog food Hud had clearly brought over for her. From time to time, Jo had Rachel over for an overnight visit. When Hud was going away with a woman for a weekend, for instance. Hunter especially enjoyed the visits. He was still working on convincing Joanne that he'd be responsible enough for his own dog. But he already had Sarah's rescue dog, Shackles, at his father's house so Joanne was in no rush for another dog. Even though Rachel was technically Hud's dog, Joanne had joint custody.

After feeding Rachel, Joanne made coffee. It was all she wanted but even that tasted rancid. She threw half of it down the sink. This wasn't going to work. "Even the coffee sucks right now, Co—Rachel."

She found her cell phone, where she assumed Hud had left it for her the night before. "Hi, Mom. I guess you heard, but listen, I didn't go to the Bahamas with Hud after all."

"What happened?"

"I got jilted but life goes on. I'll be at the shop if you need me."

"Sweetie! It's too soon. You should take some time off."

"But I don't want to." Joanne took a breath. "It's better if I stay busy. Besides, I have a wedding to pay for now."

"You're not paying for the entire wedding!"

"What am I supposed to do? Leave the vendors hanging? That's not going to improve my position in our community. And this is my town, not his. I'll take care of my obligations. Then I'll go after Chuck for his half."

Joanne hung up with her mother, then quickly texted her son that she'd decided not to go to the Bahamas and would be at the shop should he need her. Rummaging through her closet for her brightest dress, Joanne chose a tailored yellow-and-white short-sleeved dress with pockets. One of her favorite work dresses. Plus, it said, "I'm happy and well-adjusted and ready to sell you a wedding dress."

Or at least that's what she hoped it said.

Joanne was the first at the boutique and opened up the shop. She headed to the computer in the back to check the material inventory and had already pulled up some designs she'd been working on when Nora showed up.

"You're really here."

"I said I would be. There's no point in staying home. Better to keep busy. This shop is all I have now."

Nora gave Joanne a quick hug. "No use in dwelling."

"I'd be bored at home."

Not if Hud were to show up every night and pretend they were in the Bahamas. But she'd probably ruined all that by throwing up. Anyway, he was a busy firefighter and they were headed toward the height of wildfire season. She didn't need to take up all his time with her drama.

"I'm not going to be the sad jilted bride of the bad luck boutique. I'm going to be the powerful and exalted jilted bride."

"You don't have to be the jilted bride at all."

Joanne held up her index finger. "Correct! I'm *so* much more than that."

"I wondered because Hud seemed so concerned about you."

"He is. He was. He won't be anymore." Then Joanne described Hud's surprise for her the previous night. The re-creation of the Bahamas.

Nora swooned. "That's like a scene from *It's a Wonderful Life*."

"It was *pretty* wonderful." Joanne gathered up her designs, pushing the image of a shirtless Hud out of her mind. "Well, I better get to work."

A couple of hours later, Joanne stood when she heard the store's door chime. They had no fittings on the books today so this might be a new client. It was rare to have walk-ins but maybe the rumors were making people curious about the jilted bride. She'd simply have to set them straight. When Joanne reached the front of the shop, she found her mother, Ramona, and her dear and oldest friend, Iris. Both were in their mid-seventies and had been friends for decades.

"Hi, honey," her mother said. "We were just headed to lunch and I brought you something."

It appeared to be a book, and when she handed it to Joanne, she read the title: *The 7 Stages of Grieving*.

"Now, I know what you're going to say—nobody died. But a *dream* died, honey, and that's almost the same thing."

"Except that…it's not." Joanne paged through the book. "Mom, really. I'm going to be fine."

"It's horrible, what happened." Iris, a small woman with her heart in her smile, said, "I would cast a spell on him but all I can do is knit. Our friend Diane is the one who uses spells."

"She does not, *Iris*." Ramona shook her head. "She's simply into extreme positive thinking."

"As in I'm positive I'm going to cast a spell on his ass," Iris said.

Joanne actually laughed. "Thanks for coming in, but unless you need a wedding dress… I should get back to my work."

"Don't you worry," Iris said, patting her hand. "I'm going to talk K.R. into renewing our vows. Then I'll come back and have you design a wedding dress."

"Aw, that's sweet. And when that happens, I'll be here. Thanks for the book, Mom."

But she wouldn't be desperate for business if she could maintain the status quo, even given superstitious Tilly. The Taylor wedding might be Joanne's only chance to have one of her dresses appear in a magazine, as the Taylor family was high profile in Fortune. Brenda and her mother, Patricia, had loved the design ideas, calling them original and romantic.

Yes, that was her. She loved romance. Someday maybe she'd get some of it in her real life, too. But for now, she would go with keeping romance alive in her designs. Joanne designed a few dresses each year and sewed each by hand. She had an industrial sewing machine in the back of the shop and kept a second in her spare room at home. Customers loved that each dress was unique and one of a kind. Joanne strived to make it so. It meant many hours, a touch of occasional carpal tunnel and eyestrain, but the finished product was always breathtaking.

When the door chimed again later that afternoon, Joanne was both surprised and pleased to see her son. "Hey, didn't your father pick you up from school today?"

"Yeah, but I asked him if I could skate over here and bring you something." Hunter dug in his backpack.

Matt was so lenient with their son. Joanne would have preferred him not to skate all over town, even with a helmet, but she'd been trying to let go a little bit more and not be such a helicopter parent. Influenced largely by Hud, of course, who had a lot to say about teenage boys.

Hunter brought out a pink box. "To celebrate."

Joanne blinked. "Celebrate?"

"It's a cupcake from Lawson's Bakery. You can celebrate getting rid of Chuck the Douche."

Then Hunter opened the box, displaying a white frosted cupcake with drizzles of caramel sauce. Her favorite. He sang, "Na Na Hey Hey Kiss Him Goodbye." Considering this was a crowd chant at sporting events, she had to wonder how long her son had been dying to sing this to Chuck. Hunter ended the chant with a little jig and spin on his skateboard.

Nora clapped and laughed with Hunter, fist-bumping him. "Hey, little man, you're really good."

"Seriously?" Joanne didn't want anyone's pity but this wasn't good, either. "This isn't something to *celebrate*."

As a mother, she wanted to set a good example for her son and celebrating big breakups, especially when one person had been completely humiliated, didn't seem right, either. Besides, was he completely ignoring whatever feelings she might have about this, or sincerely trying to cheer her up? She took in her teenager's sharp intelligent gaze, so like his father's, and decided he meant well.

But later, they'd have a conversation about all this. She should have considered Hunter's feelings about Chuck more than she had. At the time, Hunter had been adjusting to his father separating from the Air Force and wanting more of a relationship with him. He'd gotten in trouble at school, tagging a fence with his friends, and generally been going through an "I hate everyone" stage. It had been a difficult time. She'd blamed it all on Matt re-inserting himself into Hunter's life and failed to take a deeper look at what Hunter might have noticed that she'd somehow missed.

Hunter shrugged. "Every day is a new day, or something like that. That's what you always tell me. Pick yourself up and try again. See? I listen."

Oh right. Busted. "You're right. It's a new day. I'll eat this for dessert tonight."

"Promise you'll break your diet?"

"Yeah." She'd dug into that wedding cake pretty fiercely but that was uncommon for her.

To Hunter, she was the boring parent. If it sometimes felt she'd been on a health food kick her entire life, it had actually only been the past decade. She'd banned junk food from her home because of her son. All the fun had gone out of her life, too. Then Matt had wanted to spend more time with Hunter. Now suddenly Joanne didn't have control over everything Hunter did or ate anymore, but that was simply expected since he was a teenager. Sixteen, and on his way to a driver's license. She shuddered when she thought of how a young person's life could change with one decision made in a weak moment. It was the reason she'd started talking safe sex with her son early on.

Every once in a while, though she loved her son with all her heart, she allowed herself to imagine what her life might have been like had she not been a teenage mother. Maybe she and Hudson would have gotten back together eventually and been one of those "I married my high school sweetheart" stories she loved reading about. But once she'd found out about her pregnancy, she'd had to accept that she and Hud were done forever. Her focus had to be on her son and their life together.

Being a single mom was the hardest thing she'd ever done, and though she wanted more kids, the next time she'd need a partner to rely on daily. Because she'd never want to raise a child on her own again.

"Are you absolutely sure?" Hudson stared at their probie, whose forehead had broken out in a sweat. "Be sure."

"I mean…pretty sure."

"Pretty sure is not good enough," Hudson said. "This is important. Life or death."

One more moment of intense pressure, and J.P., the probie, folded. "I'm out."

He laid his cards down on the poker table.

"Wise decision, son," Alex, the engine driver said, as he revealed his full house.

"Damn you, Alex." Hudson threw his cards. "Guess I'm dead."

Morbidly, their firehouse called their poker game

life or death. But this was nothing to some of the jokes they shared to deal with the high-pressure stakes of actual life or death.

"Let me see your cards." Alex frowned, turning them over.

He saw clearly the big fat nothing that Hud had. Then Alex turned J.P.'s cards over, revealing a better hand than Hud's. He crossed his arms, feeling a smirk coming on.

"Never play poker with LT again, J.P. You're not ready," Alex said. "Guy has the best poker face I've ever seen."

Hudson supposed that was true enough. He'd carefully calibrated his life to reveal nothing. Zero. Zip. He'd also pared life down to the bare essentials, simplifying everything: women, sex, food, sleep. In that order. Never love. Hell no. He'd tried that once, and almost wound up giving her away on her wedding day. That had been a close call. It probably didn't help that he'd never updated Jo on how he felt. How he'd apparently always feel, given that he couldn't seem to shake her no matter how hard he tried.

And he did try.

The great irony was that Hudson Decker, ladykiller and serial dater, was still hung up on his first love. Should any of his men ever find out how long he'd had it bad for her, the ribbing would never end. But damn, seeing her body so exposed shook him. He hadn't expected to feel so turned on. The way she'd looked in that two-piece swimsuit was an image he couldn't un-see. Nor did he want to. Ever. Jo always dressed conservatively in dresses and rarely even in jeans and shorts. Seeing her that close to naked had him pulling every resource he had to stay away. In her drunken state, he wondered how much she'd remember about their conversation.

Because like an idiot, he'd presented himself as an option. Shocked, she'd gazed at him through her tipsy haze. Brought up all the women he'd dated over the years. Apparently not noticed that he'd never been serious about one of them. Or maybe she *had* noticed, and figured he was still the same sixteen-year-old that broke up with her when she'd helped him discover the wonders of sex. Jackass move on his part, sure. Hud had been solidly in the friend zone for years. When Chuck had shown up in her life, Hud had tried to dissuade her from getting serious with him. But Jo claimed she was ready for something permanent, and Chuck was that safety and security she'd looked for. Hud believed that Chuck was the kind of guy who rode under the radar with women, a player who wasn't obvious about it. In other words, an expert.

The station alarm went off, announcing a house fire. Everyone moved lightning fast, Hud nearly kicking the poker table out of his way. It was wildfire season and a simple house fire could mean disaster depending on the location. Using the laptop he used as the LT, Hudson scoped out the address, relieved to see the home was located in town and not near any open fields. Fortune being a town with strict growth guidelines set by the city council years ago, there were still dry, open parcels of land in the strangest of places. Next to a liquor store. Abutted to a block of single-family homes. It made wildfire season particularly dicey around Wildfire Ridge.

Speaking through their headsets, they exchanged information on the closest fire hydrant and prepared the process. Hud would access point of entry. The rest of the crew would fall back and set up hoses and the engine ladder if needed. But when they pulled up to the address, a senior citizen stood on the front lawn appearing in zero distress. She waved at them happily.

Hudson had a bad feeling about this.

"It's Widow Diaz," Alex said.

"Crap." Hudson exited first and met her on the lawn. "Where's the fire?"

"It's Puggy. Poor baby is stuck under the house again. I knew you wouldn't come unless I said I had a fire."

"Mrs. Diaz, you can't keep doing this," Hudson chastised while he waved to the others the all clear. "We've talked about this."

"I know, but I can't stand his pitiful wailing."

"Told you to call *me* next time, and not the entire fire department."

But his warnings wouldn't work when she knew that Hudson wasn't going to report her as wasting the town's valuable resources. Growing up, she'd been like a grandmother to him.

"I would have called you, but I knew you were at work."

Hud pulled off his gear. "This is the last time."

With that, Hudson crawled under the house, calling the ridiculous name. "Puggy." It was worse than Coco. The stupid senseless dog hadn't yet figured out that he could get stuck down here while chasing whatever critter he was after. A terror mix, oh excuse him, *terrier* mix, he had anxiety issues and liked to bite the hand that rescued him. Swearing and cursing, Hud met all of the spiders, using his flashlight to shine the light on their little homes. Thank God he wasn't an arachnophobe. Or claustrophobic.

"C'mere, you SOB." Hud reached the dog and tugged on his collar, hauling him out. "I've told you this before, but I'll say it again. If you get in, you can get out."

Hud emerged with Puggy and handed him over to Mrs. Diaz. "Last time, right?"

She accepted her dog happily. "Oh thank you, Hudson. You're the sweetest boy. I knew that from the time you were six years old. I don't care how big or tall you are, you're still my sweet boy. And if you come over tomorrow, I'll have brownies for you."

Now *that* he would welcome. No one ever baked

for him. His parents had retired to Florida. Jo was a complete health nut and the women he dated weren't interested in domesticity.

A large part of the reason he dated them.

"Look into that chicken wire fence we talked about before," Hudson said as he waved goodbye and joined the guys, who were all checking their phones.

"Back to the station," Hudson said, gathering up the gear he'd taken off and carrying it back to the truck.

"Oh no. Here comes trouble. It's our favorite badge bunny, but she only has eyes for Hud." Alex snorted.

"Wow," J.P. the probie breathed, staring over Hudson's shoulder.

Hudson turned to watch Grace Smoker walking toward them. "Wow" was right. She was gorgeous, long dark straight hair down to her back. Long legs that she had no compunction in displaying often, in short shorts that left little to the imagination. Today she wore a pair of those shorts with a tight tie-dyed tank top. It was the kind she made and regularly sold at the Mushroom Mardi Gras in town every year.

"Hey, guys," she said. "Everything okay here?"

"We're good," Hudson said. "Packing it up now."

"Thanks, whatever you did." She reached up to touch his shoulder.

Funny, he felt... Nothing.

That's because I want Jo. I can't think of any-one but her.

Except he didn't want to be the rebound guy, did he? Did it count when he was also the first guy? Maybe all the others had been the rebound guys. Well, he could tell himself that. Wouldn't necessarily make it true. All this time, Jo had been looking for stability in her life and he'd been waiting, he supposed.

"Do me a favor?" Hud asked Grace now as he heard the engine ladder start up.

"Anything," she breathed.

"Check in on her every once in a while." He nudged his chin in the direction of Mrs. Diaz's home. "She's alone too much."

"Did she call you about Puggy?" Grace went hand on hip and tossed her hair back. "I told her not to bother you. You have real fires to attend to. It's wildfire season."

"Wait. She asked *you* for help first?"

She had the decency to look chastised and stuck out her lower lip. "There are spiders under there."

Hud had a little shiver of the unwelcome kind. She looked ridiculous and sounded even meaner. Not that he'd expect her to crawl under there herself, but how about calling on one of the many men who would love nothing more than to please her? Hudson had heard she was dating the new deputy in town. She could have called him, but then again, maybe she'd wanted Mrs. Diaz to call the fire department out. There were so many problems with that, Hud didn't know where to begin. First, Grace knew better. She wasn't helpless. Far from it.

And she was still standing in front of him, waiting.

He scratched at his chin. "Something I can do for you, Grace?"

"Now that you mention it, how about that date you keep promising me?"

"Yeah, how about it, LT?" Alex yelled. "Let's get going. Ask her out and get it over with."

J.P. was suddenly at Hudson's elbow. "Or if you're not interested…" He cleared his throat. "Sir."

"Aw, aren't you cute?" Grace winked. "But Hudson and I have a little thing going on."

"We do not."

Hudson clapped J.P. on the back and pushed him back to the rig. "We're on the city's dime. Make your dates on your own time, probie."

And with that, Hud hopped on the rig and they drove away.

Chapter Six

A week past the wedding that never was, the phone calls checking to see whether the boutique was still open had dwindled to one per day. Some thought she'd never recover from the shock and might seek a different profession. Otherwise, how could she get through each day surrounded by all the reminders? She assured everyone that no, she wasn't selling the shop, she was fine, working hard on new designs and ready to sew her butt off.

Today she wore her cool navy blue sweater dress with the short fleurette-covered sleeves and ties. It had a figure flattering defined waist. Joanne required all of her fashion mojo today because she'd moved up her appointment with the Taylors. She wanted to talk about fittings. They'd have to select from the designs she'd prepared for them soon and Joanne wanted to get to work right away. She had a feeling the wedding gown would take her months to get perfect for Brenda.

Hud still checked in with her every day via text, but he hadn't dropped by since the night he'd re-created the beach scene. Since the night she'd made a fool out of herself drinking too much and wearing too little.

She planned on calling him soon and suggesting a night bingeing on whatever current action-adventure series he was hooked on.

"Good morning," Nora said, when Joanne waltzed in carrying two cups of coffee from The Drip. "Is that coffee?"

"Just how you like it. Plenty of foam." Joanne handed Nora's over. "Tired?"

"Taking my work home with me," Nora said with a yawn. "I sewed every single pearl on Tilly's sleeves last night."

"I bet it looks wonderful."

They got to work, talking over the Taylor wedding and whether or not they'd also be entrusted with the bridesmaid's dresses, too. Two hours later, the Taylors didn't show for their appointment.

"This doesn't make any sense. They'd wanted to get in earlier, so I rescheduled."

"Maybe there was a mix-up," Nora said with a shrug. "You should call them."

"I will." But neither Brenda nor Patricia answered their phone, so Joanne left them each a message. Maybe they planned on keeping their first appointment after all, but it was rude not to call or show-up.

The rest of the morning progressed easily, with a visit from Eve, who came by to work on their website and back up their system. Just the thought that Joanne could lose any of her designs kept her awake some nights. Eve was a wiz with anything software related. After Eve left, Jill Davis showed up. Joanne had designed and sewed a sweetheart collar satin dress for the bride-to-be, but the alterations weren't quite done. They had it on the schedule, but Jill wasn't in any rush because the wedding had been postponed to after wildfire season. Since she owned the outdoor adventures camp on Wildfire Ridge and wanted to be married there, it made sense to wait a couple more months.

"Don't worry. I don't expect it to be done yet." Jill smiled. "I just…want to see it again."

"I understand." Joanne led her to the back of the boutique and carefully took her dress down. "Still in love with it?"

"I dream about it," Jill said, beaming.

"The day will be here soon."

"Three months. Three long months." She glanced

at Joanne. "I was so sorry to hear about…what happened. Are you okay?"

Joanne dismissed it with a wave. "I'm fine. These things happen."

Although that wasn't exactly true. She racked her brain to come up with the name of a bride, any bride, that she'd ever known to be jilted.

She came up with no one, but this was a small town.

"Oh good. I'm glad you're okay. Because I was going to ask about colors for cummerbunds. The tux is black and Sam will wear anything I tell him to wear."

"Good man." Joanne led her to the color swatches. "Oh my. This green would really bring out Hud's eyes."

"Sam's eyes are blue," Jill said, disregarding the fact Joanne had called her fiancé by another man's name. "The most beautiful dark blue."

Quickly, Joanne paged to the blue colors. What was wrong with her lately? "I forgot Hud has blue eyes."

"Sam," Jill said kindly and a bit dreamily.

Oh. My. God. This had to stop. She had to get Hudson out of her head! Like now.

Jill, caught in her own little world, thank God, went on. "I'm going to be Jill Davis-Hawker. Or maybe just Jill Hawker. I haven't made up my mind yet."

"I say go with Jill Hawker," Nora said, glaring at Joanne. "*Sam* and Jill Hawker. I love it."

Jill sighed.

"Sam," Joanne repeated. *SamSamSamSam*.

Hudson.

After Jill left, Nora turned to Joanne, hands on hips. "Want to tell me what's going on?"

Joanne didn't know where to begin. "I wish I knew. It's just…something happened."

"I'm guessing it has to do with Hud."

"The other night, and the Bahamas re-creation."

"That sounded very sweet but Hud has always done nice things like that for you. Right?"

Yes, he had. But again, this had seemed different. Physical and intense. At least on her part. "I kind of…lingered on his back when I put suntan lotion over it. And he has a pretty amazing back."

Nora wrinkled her nose. "I'm sorry? You put suntan lotion on? Inside?"

"Yes! We really got into our re-creation."

"That's for sure."

"And I wore my red bikini."

The significance of that statement would not be lost on Nora. Joanne had specifically chosen that bikini to seduce her husband. Nora had helped her pick it out. Joanne had others, too, to be worn in *public*. She tended to be conservative and the red suit was not.

"Why would you wear that one unless you…" Nora quirked a brow.

"I know! Why did I? And why do I keep *thinking* about him? This is ridiculous. I was just jilted and the last thing I need is another rocky relationship. And Hud and I… Well, we didn't work before."

"When you were sixteen, you mean?" Nora crossed her arms and smirked. "Shock."

"The thing is, I obviously wanted him to see me in the swimsuit." Joanne closed her eyes. "Maybe I wanted to feel attractive again. Desirable."

"Or maybe you have the hots for your best friend. Because seriously, he's the total package. Looks, personality, rockin' body, charm, everything. And, in case you haven't noticed, Joanne, he's *crazy* about you."

Those words hit her in unexpected quiet and private places she didn't often explore anymore. Now it felt like a thread had been pulled. She was no longer able to ignore that there was still a pull between them. A connection. But there was a good reason they weren't together. Make that a few good reasons.

"No. He isn't. And he might be the total package, but he's never been serious about anyone. That tells me he's still not ready to settle down with one woman. Maybe not even capable of it. At least, that's what I suggested to him when he brought it up."

"When he brought *what* up?"

"Oh, I guess I forgot that part. Did I mention I'd

been drinking on an empty stomach? Hud started in on me on how I pick the wrong men. I reminded him of my reasonable wish list. He told me he fits every item on it." She took a breath. "And he does."

Nora smiled, wider this time. "In-te-res-ting."

"That's when I told him that he's excluded because he's my best friend *and* he likes women. Too many of them. He took great offense to that."

"Look, it sounds like you two need to talk."

"We're avoiding each other, I think. I miss my best friend. But now I have a problem because I just noticed he's superhot."

"Seriously? You *just* noticed this?"

"It's kind of like I wore blinders for years when it came to Hud. I tried not to think about him... sexually."

But ever since those sinewy muscles bunched under her fingertips... Maybe it had been the alcohol, the beach re-creation, or the way he looked in those board shorts.

"He takes care of me," Joanne said. "And it would be too easy to get sucked into thinking that it's more than a friendship. I can't do that to myself. I've been through enough. What I need now is security. Safety. So, I'm going to forget about relationships for a while and focus on business."

"I say go for it!" Nora said. "Whatever it turns into, a fling or forever, you two will get through it. Nothing will ever destroy your friendship."

Joanne wished that were true. But even if this wasn't the "bad luck boutique" it wasn't the "good luck boutique," either.

She'd have to continue to make her own luck.

Hud was in the meeting from hell. Seated across from him in his office was Chief Fire Inspector Richard Ferguson, Battalion Chief Kevin Murphy and Sheriff Ryan Davis. They had just entered the height of wildfire season with brush fires in remote forest areas that were spreading due to high winds and had reason to be concerned. California wildfire season didn't peak in the summertime. It peaked in September and October, following the dry season and before the start of their rainy one.

Wildfire Ridge was known for wildfires, hence the name, but they'd been controlled for years. A few months ago, one of the deputies had caught a kid throwing a lit rag into a Dumpster and they'd arrested their teenage firebug. Since then, it could be said they were all a little skittish. A house fire, even an accidental car fire could be disastrous, but more often than not, all that was required was high winds, hellish heat, open land and dry tinder.

On top of all that, due to budget cuts they had a huge shortage of federal firefighters. So, they were all doing what they could with state and county Cal Fire. Hud was already shorthanded due to a few of his men traveling to volunteer at the latest forest fire outside of Yosemite. To compound matters, the in-spector wanted to discuss the latest place not fit to pass his airtight inspection, a local restaurant.

It was not a good day to be Hudson Decker.

A message flashed across his phone and he glanced at it in the middle of Ferguson's diatribe.

Jo: Movie tonight after your shift? I'll let you pick what we watch but I'm picking up fish tacos for din-ner.

Yeah, so eventually he'd learned to appreciate *fish* tacos. Jo said fish was good for his heart. The irony wasn't lost on him, since she's the one who had bro-ken it in the first place. But that was years ago. They were both kids.

He hadn't gone to her house in a few days, giving her space. But she'd officially gone back to work full-time, a good sign. She was moving on from "two-buck" Chuck. Now the question was whether or not she would be ready to move on with Hud into brand-new territory. Jo and Hud, the reboot. It wasn't that crazy an idea. He wouldn't screw it up again this time.

Because the night of the beach recreation, some-thing had shifted between them. And he'd made a surprising decision. This time he wasn't putting his best friend back together so some other man could have her. This was his moment.

After the tense meeting, which gave him a thousand action items, Hud got back to his crew and made them go through drills. J.P. needed them more than anyone else, but they could all benefit from the practice.

Later, done with his forty-eight-hour shift, Hud showered and changed at the station. By the time he got to Jo's, the sun had started to ebb. He found her sitting on one of the steps leading to her porch, dressed in a short blue dress, her mood seeming to match the color.

He took a seat on the step next to her. "What's wrong?"

She turned to him and the absolute look of despair in her eyes drop-kicked his stomach. "I think my shop is going to be known as the bad luck boutique."

"That's ridiculous. What does that even mean?"

"It means I'm bad luck to prospective brides. The Taylors didn't show up, and people are calling to ask if I'm okay and still open for business."

"Maybe they thought you'd gone on the honeymoon without him."

She seemed to consider it. "No. It's just in the way they talk to me. The pity. Today at the fish taco place, the waitress hugged me and cried. Cried! I don't want to be known as the jilted bride, owner of the bad luck boutique."

He took her hand and squeezed it. "And you won't be. It may take people a little time. Why would they think one has anything to do with the other? I don't get that."

"That's because you're a man and you don't know how superstitious brides are about their wedding day."

"How superstitious are we talking?"

"Some down to the date they pick to get married. A lucky number." She sighed. "How am I supposed to convince everyone that I've got good luck again?"

"Start dating someone new." Even though that was in his best interest, he didn't see how it could hurt the situation. "Be happy and show it."

"Who should I date?"

"Me."

She pulled back, searching his eyes. "You're not teasing me."

"No. I mean this. I'm putting myself in the running."

"You…and me?"

"Besides the fact that I do make every one of your list requirements, I also know how you take your coffee. Exactly three tablespoons of soy milk. I know that you prefer that your vanilla ice cream and chocolate brownie cake never touch each other, lest they contaminate each other."

"If I'm going to splurge on cake and ice cream, which I only do with you, I need to take my time and enjoy them—"

"Individually."

She laughed, and he didn't miss the fact that she shifted closer to him, so that they now sat hip to hip. "I'm sorry for what I said the other night."

"I get it. I'm sure I don't seem like the most stable guy when it comes to relationships."

"Not with your recent past. But could you... I mean, do you think you can be exclusive? With someone?" She set her hand on his thigh.

Jo's signature move. He recognized it, and his skin hadn't felt this tight in over a decade. Working out as much as he did, his heart never spiked anymore the way it did now.

He swallowed. "With you? Yeah, I could. Definitely."

Exclusivity would not be difficult with Jo. Not when he'd watched her date other men over the years, realizing that she might be with him if only their timing hadn't been so off.

She smiled. Then she leaned toward him, closer, till she was nearly in his lap. He would have taken the lead, but he wanted, he needed this to be her idea. She had to be sure because they weren't going back. Not if he had anything to do with it. He'd make this work. This time he was ready for them. For her. It would be his mission to prove it. One hand in his hair, she tugged his lips to hers and kissed him. Letting her take the lead, he then responded with the fierceness his body felt at having her so close. She opened to him and their tongues tangled in a blazing heat.

She broke the kiss and they simply stared at each other for several seconds.

"Well, that's still there, isn't it?" Jo finally said.

"I didn't have any doubts." He pressed his forehead to hers. "You asked me if I could be exclusive and I gave you the truth. Now let me ask you something. Are you ready to try this again, you and me? Because I won't be your rebound guy."

"I understand how you feel," she whispered. "But you won't be the rebound guy because you were the *first* guy."

"And I screwed that up. It won't happen again."

"Hud, if you felt this way, why didn't you say something sooner?" She pulled back to meet his gaze.

He wasn't sure even he knew the answer to that question. Jo had seemed happy enough without him, focused primarily on her son for years. Easier not to rock the boat, and yeah, fear, large and gripping, that he'd hurt her again or she'd hurt him. That maybe deep down he didn't know *how* to love her.

"Maybe it had to be the right moment." But he wasn't letting her off easy. "What about you?"

"I don't know. It didn't seem possible for so long. We didn't want the same things. You never seemed interested in slowing down…with all of your dating.

And family is important to me. I always have to put my son first."

"Family is important to me, too."

Hud's parents had moved to Florida, but he still visited them every chance he could. He was a late-in-life child with no siblings and had been somewhat spoiled. But he didn't blame his parents for any of that. It had taken Hud a while to grow up and realize how much his actions affected others. That decisions he'd made in the heat of the moment would affect the rest of his life.

Jo had felt like family because she'd been a part of his life for so many years. Hunter felt like his family, too.

Hud loved Jo's son, but he was still sensitive about Matt Conner. Hud understood he was a good guy and had never shirked from his responsibilities toward Jo and their son. But it was still difficult to be around him at times because he'd been the one to permanently alter Jo's life. She'd changed because of him, as their child grew inside her.

And Matt didn't even love Joanne. Never had.

"I loved the way you took care of Hunter like he was the only thing that mattered in your world. You gave everything up for him."

"Maybe I gave up too much. When it was finally time for my own life to begin again, I had an emotional disconnection in my brain. I told myself who

I *should* want. Who was safe. Not necessarily who I really wanted."

She met his gaze, squeezed his thigh.

He kissed her then, to seal it. To set in stone this was their second chance. Neither one of them came to this relationship as a blank slate. Not the way they'd been the first time. To his mind, this would only make them richer. Fuller. As long as they could shut the rest of the world out.

The kiss grew passionate, wild and hot. He tugged her closer, not able to get her close enough. Hud got hard, and he wanted in the house before they became someone's adult entertainment.

"Inside," he said, as he pulled her to her feet.

"Yes."

"Mom?"

They both froze on the top step and turned to the sidewalk.

The annoyed-sounding word had come out of Hunter, who now stood at the bottom of the first step, glaring at Hud. "What's going on?"

Jo pulled out of his arms. "Hud came by to…to…"

"Kiss your mother," Hud finished, not letting go of her hand.

"Gross!"

"Honey, what are you *doing* here?" Jo asked.

"Forgot my History textbook," he said, storming past them. He slammed the screen door shut.

Jo sagged into Hud's open arms. "Oh my God.

He's been at his father's all this time and he just now comes to get his textbook?"

He chuckled. "I think we have a bigger problem."

"Yes, but I'm trying to ignore that."

"He'll get over it." His hand slid down her back, not wanting to give up contact just yet. But he'd have to leave her alone to deal with Hunter. He knew her well enough to know that she'd want it that way.

"I know, I know. Kids are resilient and all that." She met his gaze. "What do I tell him?"

"Tell him he's not scaring me away. No matter how hard he tries. I'm not going anywhere."

"Oh, Hud." She clung to him and he crushed her against his chest. "Is this really happening?"

"Yeah, and it's about time. Now go inside, talk to your son, and I'll see you tomorrow."

And with that he gave her one last kiss, then watched her walk inside before he headed home, happier than he could recall feeling in a decade.

Chapter Seven

"Hunter Matthew Conner!"

Now that Joanne was out of Hud's arms, she could think straight again. Her son had been incredibly rude to a man who'd been like a second father to him. Yes, sure, it had to have been a bit of a surprise to see her and Hud in a passionate embrace. She was a little embarrassed by that, because it had all gone out of control so quickly. But that's how it had once been between them and nothing had changed.

Hunter appeared in the doorway to his bedroom, holding a textbook. "Did he leave?"

"Yes, and did you have to be so rude to him? He's always been good to you. Taught you how to ride a bicycle, all the things your father didn't do because he wasn't around. Hud deserves a little more respect from you."

"Why? Is he going to be your *guy* now that Chuck's finally gone?"

Joanne crossed her arms. "I'm sorry you caught us like that, but I'm not going to discuss my love life with my teenage son. It's none of your business."

"Okay, great. Then it's none of your business that I'm going to enlist in the U.S. Marine Corps as soon as I graduate. I talked to Sam about it and he's going to give me some advice."

Hunter had brought out the heavy ammunition. His unrelenting desire to drive her to an early grave with worry. She'd thought it was just a stage but now she was concerned there was far more to her son's fascination with the military than a few video games. And no wonder. Their small town was filled with returning servicemen, including their sheriff, a Medal of Honor recipient.

"You should talk to Hud. He was a soldier, too." Hud would talk some sense into him. He'd do it for Joanne.

"And my dad was an Airman. But I'm still going to be a Marine."

"No need to rush into anything." Refusing to be intimidated, Joanne held her ground. "You'll apologize to Hud next time you see him."

"Fine!" Hunter threw his textbook on the couch.

"But I don't get why you need anyone. It's always been you and me and we did fine. Then Chuck the Douche came along and ruined everything. Now, you're going to date *Hud*? He's like my uncle, so that means he's...like your brother or something."

Joanne ignored that. Hud was nothing like a brother to Joanne and never had been. But she couldn't fault her son for operating in the dark with the little information he had. He'd been spared from the family drama of their past. The child who turned their three lives upside down didn't have to know the deep and complicated history she'd had with Hud. With Matt. He didn't have to know that in an alternate reality, she would have preferred for Hud to be his father and not Matt.

The words as to why she needed someone special in her life were on the tip of her tongue, but she couldn't say them.

You're leaving me soon. Whether it's the Marines or college, you're no longer a child. Pretty soon you won't need me at all. I need to have my own life. I want to be happy and in love again. Now I finally have a second chance with Hud.

"Let me drive you back to your dad's house." Joanne got her purse and keys.

"Maybe I could drive," Hunter said.

It was a calculated move on his part, made at a time when he thought he might have some leverage with her. He'd gotten his driver's permit, but the driving hours had been limited to rides with his father. Joanne was terrified of being in the car with Hunter at the wheel. She had to get over this fear but letting go was difficult. Her son was nearly a man now, as tall as his father. She'd lost an argument that Hunter shouldn't get his driver's license until he was seventeen, when teenage fatality rates dropped significantly. She'd done the research. But Hunter didn't want to hear about it, and he'd gotten Matt to side with him.

"Um…" Never let it be said that she wasn't any good at stalling.

"I've driven with everybody but you. I even drove with Sarah the other day. Really, Mom, I'm a good driver."

"I'm sure you are." She gnawed at her lower lip, chewing the rest of the lipstick off. Even Hud agreed that Joanne should let her son drive her a few places around town. Said it would ease her fears to see that he knew what he was doing.

Or reinforce her fears.

Still, she was surrounded on all sides by men who wanted her to let Hunter grow up. And she supposed that if she wanted him to respect the choices she made, she would have to start trusting him a little, too.

Like with her life. Gulp.

She tossed him the keys. "You're driving the speed limit and not a mile above it."

He caught the keys midair. "Hells yeah!"

Joanne strapped into her seat belt and made sure that Hunter did the same. She stuck out her hand. "Give me your phone."

"Why? It's in my pocket. Like I'm going to text with you sitting right next to me?" He snorted.

Her hand hadn't moved from its position. "I'll make sure you're not distracted by it buzzing in your pocket."

He pulled it out of his pants pocket and set it in her hand. "Here. Where's the trust?"

The fact he'd made such a big deal out of it told her that Matt and Sarah weren't insisting he do the same. Well, she'd have to address that issue with them at some point. Still, Hunter did drive reasonably well even if she did correct his position, reminding him to keep his hands at ten and two o'clock. Finally, thank you God, they arrived at Matt and Sarah's residence, and Joanne hopped out of the passenger door and came around the side.

"Thanks, Mom. I did okay, yeah?" Hunter climbed out and immediately put his hand out for his phone.

"You did. I'm very impressed at your speed limit consistency." She handed his phone over, bussed his cheek and had to stand on tiptoes and stretch to do so.

Once she was seated in the driver's seat, Hunter leaned in the window. "Sorry I said it was gross for Hud to be kissing you."

"That's okay. I understand this is tough for you.

And I don't know what's going to happen with me and Hud. This is all very new. It's just that you need to know... I *really* like him."

"I like him, too. He's hella better than Chuck for sure, but I still don't think you should date him."

Yeah, she didn't think it would be that easy. She nodded. "And you have a right to your opinion."

"Okay, then." He turned to go. "See ya!"

"Aren't you forgetting something?" She reached back and handed him the textbook.

He looked sheepish, accepting it. "Thanks."

"Study hard!"

Joanne started up the car and took off, wondering if Hunter really needed that textbook or if he'd come over to check up on her.

Here were a few vital facts about Joanne Michelle Brandt:

She loved lists.

She loved order.

Early on, she'd planned how many children she would have: girl, boy, girl. In that order.

College would be somewhere far away, preferably New York City, where she would study fashion design.

She'd wanted to marry Hudson Decker from the moment she laid eyes on him.

And when she was sixteen years old, she blew up her entire life plan.

So much for planning. How did the saying go? Life is what happens when you're busy making all your plans—or something like that. Joanne did not marry Hudson Decker, she did not go away for college, and she had one child, a boy. So far. And if she ever had any more, she now knew they would not be with a weasel-face, loser, no good, useless man like Chuck Ellis! Good riddance.

Yes, she was finally pissed. Beyond pissed. She didn't know which stage of grief she'd entered, but the anger that woke with her every morning was palpable. She felt it wrap around her neck and squeeze. She wanted to find Chuck, and—well, she didn't know what yet, but it was going to hurt him like hell. He was going to pay her back for every last cent she'd spent on the wedding. No, not even his *half* anymore, because it was his fault the wedding hadn't happened. That wasn't unreasonable.

And yet, when she thought that she'd be *married* to him now if he had shown up—that's when she got really spooked. She'd almost made the biggest mistake of her life. Because she didn't want to wind up alone. Now she had Hud again, telling her he wanted to make this thing work between them. He wasn't going anywhere—his words. It was like living her first dream, brought back to life. A dream she was too afraid to believe now because by now she understood plans didn't work out most of the time. But she and Hud, they *had* something. They always had. They had to work this time. Hunter would get over it, and as for everyone else? Of course, they'd be supportive.

When Matt married Sarah, Joanne's mother had finally given up on her hopes that eventually Joanne would do the right thing and marry the father of her son. *Thank you, Matt.*

Joanne had been kneeling for several minutes in the back of the shop working on Jill's wedding dress train and she rose now, rubbing her lower back. Her phone buzzed, and she reached for it to read a text from Hud:

Silver Saddle, tonight.

She smiled. Once, she'd thought of Hud as the love of her life, but for the past several years he'd been the fun of her life. If she was too tired to go out, he'd find an activity too difficult to resist. She hadn't been dancing in a long time.

She responded:

Maybe.

Hud: That wasn't a question.

"Sometimes I can't believe this is really happening," Joanne said to Nora, when she entered their back room, holding a dress wrapped in plastic. "Me and Hud."

Of course, she'd updated her friend and partner on everything: the kiss, the interruption, the talk with her son. Hud's revelation.

"I understand. To hear Hud say he'll be exclusive would shock anyone."

Panic tore through Joanne. "Why? You don't think he can do it?"

Nora held up her palm in the universal Stop sign. "Whoa, calm down. I didn't *say* that."

"But maybe he can't. And maybe it's too soon for me to be out in public kicking up my heels. I might be seen as coldhearted to be over Chuck so soon."

"Excuse me, but I thought the whole idea was to show everyone how over him you are and how happy you are now. The boutique depends on it. You want to set everyone straight. This is a good thing, not a bad thing. You've come to your senses and thank goodness Chuck stood you up. And I might add that just being seen with Hud is sort of a good luck charm."

All of that might be true, and Joanne was definitely over Chuck. Like a veil had been lifted from her eyes she saw why Hud and even Matt hadn't liked him. He was arrogant, told stories about himself in the third person and liked to feel sorry for himself. "Chuck didn't get picked for the first round of the draft." Morose, he'd fish for compliments. She couldn't think of a single redeeming quality about Chuck, other than the fact that he was reasonably good-looking, and he'd been immediately interested in a commitment and settling down. Having kids.

Frankly, she was going to give herself a pass because he was gone so much on the road with his minor league team that every time she saw him she'd forgotten what irritated her about him. He'd always been on his best behavior with her, but he'd never been in Hud's league. It's just that she'd believed for a time she was also out of Hud's league, other than as a best friend.

She'd seen the women he dated. All model types and beauty queens. She'd turned into a boring single mother with a teenage kid and that didn't attract a whole lot of good men. It certainly hadn't attracted Hud, or so she'd thought.

But if she felt the pressure, the importance of making this work, what could that be doing to Hud? "He wants to take me to the Silver Saddle tonight."

"And he's such a good dancer, too."

"He's pretty proud of that." He'd spent much of his time on the dance floor collecting women's phone numbers.

She definitely didn't like thinking of all the women he'd been with, serious or not. There were bound to be comparisons. She'd always found the women nice enough, but Joanne was not in the mood to be compared to anyone.

She changed the subject. "Have the Taylors returned any of our calls?"

"No," Nora said, frowning.

It was official. They were avoiding Joanne. Whether or not it was because they suddenly hated her designs and had found someone else, or they'd bought into unfounded wedding superstitions, there was no way of knowing without first talking to them. If they were going to go with another designer, the least they could do was pull up their big girl panties and tell Joanne.

"I don't understand. They paid for my designs. We just need their final choice and we need to start sewing soon. It's rude not to at least return my calls."

"Agreed. Listen, let's talk about this tomorrow. Tonight, you go dancing." Nora rubbed Joanne's back. "You deserve it."

Nora was right. Joanne picked up her phone and texted back.

See you there, cowboy.

Dancing a little bit never hurt anyone.

Hud had spent his day off doing handyman jobs around his house and looking in on his next-door elderly neighbor, Mrs. Suarez. When he'd been gone, she'd left a note pinned to his door that her thermostat was broken.

She owned the home so there wasn't a landlord to call, and her children didn't live nearby. Hud looked in on her and took care of odd jobs around the house.

"I think I need a new one," Mrs. Suarez said. "I went to turn on the heater and...nothing."

Granted, as they moved toward autumn their nights were cooler but Hud didn't think it was time to turn on the heater. They were still having some 80 plus degree weather during the day. Still, Mrs. Suarez was on a blood thinner, so she got cold easier. He would suggest she put on a sweater, but instead he would fix the thermostat.

She was already digging through her purse when Hud tapped on it and realized she probably just needed a new battery.

Mrs. Suarez handed him a 100-dollar bill. "And keep the change, mijo."

"No need. Think you just need a new battery."

She blinked. "It takes batteries?"

He smiled. "I've got some next door."

"Let me pay you for them." She tried shoving the bill in his direction but he wasn't taking one cent from a widow on social security.

"I'll be right back with some batteries."

"Ay, que Dios te bendiga. Es un angel."

Hud wished he understood Spanish. She seemed

to think he should. He smiled and nodded. He recognized "Dios" in there, meaning "God" so he figured it couldn't be bad.

A few minutes later he'd replaced the batteries, accepted some fresh baked cookies, and moved on to replacing the sheetrock in his laundry room. Rachel had once trapped herself in there for a few hours and tried to gnaw her way out.

Ever since he'd adopted her, it seemed like his house was falling apart. Like Jo, he had a list now. It involved everything he had to replace because Rachel had either chewed it, shit or peed on it. He almost didn't have enough time to fix all the damage.

He took a bite of his cookie and picked up a new piece of cut sheetrock. Rachel belly crawled to him, sniffing, as she always did when she smelled food.

"*My* cookie. Haven't you done enough damage here?"

She sighed as if wounded and lay on the floor beside him.

Lately on his days off he'd been picking up a shift or two as one of the guides at Wildfire Ridge Outdoor Adventures. He'd been a regular on the ridge where it was situated. As part of the team that performed regular controlled burns, he'd made friends with the owner, Jill Davis, and her fiancé, who both ran the place. Jill had opened the business this summer and hired former military men as guides. Hud had been a regular on the zip lines and rock climbing.

When Sam casually asked if Hud would like to take a shift on his days off, he'd jumped at the chance.

Yeah, he usually took it easy on his days off or managed to have fun. Ride his motorcycle, zip line, rock climb. For the most part, he'd enjoyed being solo. Accepted it. He was a free and single man, after all, unencumbered by obligations. By family. He'd had plenty of money, enough to put some away for the future. That's the way he'd enjoyed life for years. And that had been enough until recently.

But today, no matter what he did around the house, sheetrock or stuck sliding glass door, he thought of Joanne. The night before when *she'd* kissed him first. He hadn't expected that. But she'd opened the door and he'd waltzed right in. And he'd been just as gob-smacked by that kiss as the first time he'd ever seen her, convinced at the time that he'd never seen anything more beautiful in his life. She'd had her blond hair longer then and an easy friendly smile. Everyone loved her. She was wicked smart and voted Most Likely to Succeed at Anything.

He'd taken care of her virginity and his in the same night. Not a cross to bear for him, to be sure, but the act had meant a lot more to her. She'd told him she loved him and started to plan their lives together. It freaked him out. Seeking distance, he'd broken up with her. Temporarily, he'd said, trying to be reasonable.

Both were too young. Blah blah blah. Well, he'd

been sixteen, so he no longer blamed himself. Much. And he'd started to date immediately, to show her that he'd meant what he said. Next thing he knew, she'd been on a date with the big man on campus, Matt Conner. He was the male version of Joanne. Successful at everything he attempted. Highly intelligent. Headed straight to the Ivy Leagues.

Then Joanne got pregnant and decided she would keep the baby. Hud was hurt and pissed, though he had no right to be. He hadn't planned on their breakup lasting forever, hadn't planned much of anything at all, actually. Forever, or so it seemed to his teenage brain, happened anyway.

When he realized he'd lost all hope of a future with Joanne, he'd driven too fast one night, lost control, and crashed his father's car. The injuries hadn't killed him, but they'd acquainted him with the fire and rescue department of Fortune Valley. He'd spent two weeks in the hospital and Jo came to visit nearly every day. She hadn't made excuses or blamed him for pushing her away. In classic Jo fashion, she took on all the responsibility and said she'd be having a child earlier than planned. That she didn't love Matt Conner. She wasn't marrying him. But obviously, she was going to be very busy for the next few years.

But she'd forever be Hud's friend.

Finished with the sheetrock, Hud picked up his tools and cleaned up.

Joanne had never mentioned the *L* word to him

again. He hadn't deserved her love anyway. Not after what he'd done. They graduated, Joanne had her son and Hud joined the Army. He went to fight because from that point on and for years, he'd been a pretty angry dude. Angry at himself. Angry at the world. He'd concluded war would give him a good place to channel all that aggression.

Yeah, he was *that* stupid.

Thank God for years and maturity because even though he'd never been in a serious relationship, he was probably healthier emotionally than most people he knew. There were no lies or deceit between him and other women. No false encouragement or games. Every relationship was always aboveboard and neat. Compartmentalized. There were months he'd go without a woman and he was good with that, too.

He'd learned to be the supportive always-single friend to Jo. He learned to push any desire for her out of his mind and heart. Mostly, it hadn't worked. He'd just faked it well because she was too important to him. Too important to cut out of his life. Any other guy in his position he'd call lame for accepting scraps, but Hud took whatever Jo was willing to give him. For years it had been a deep friendship that only made him love her more.

Yeah, he loved her. Still.

It didn't hurt to admit it anymore, which had to mean he'd made some kind of progress.

Chapter Eight

Hud arrived at the Silver Saddle, the only honky-tonk in their small town. Though many of his friends and some of the women he'd previously dated tried to drag him inside, he made excuses and said he'd see them later. He paced outside until Jo showed up and he walked to her car to meet her. This night would be special because he had plans. Plans to show her that he was in 100 percent. With no regrets.

She looked damned sexy wearing her cowgirl boots and a white sleeveless dress with a full skirt that hit above her knees. Already she was killing him, and they weren't even on the dance floor.

"C'mon," he said, taking her hand.

"Big news." She walked beside him. "I let Hunter drive with me the other night."

He stopped. "Finally?"

"It wasn't as bad as I thought it would be. You're right—it's nice to see that he knows what he's doing. But I'm still worried because of the texting and driving thing. Every teenager believes they're invincible."

He didn't particularly like the flow of this conversation, which sounded too much like a rehashing of their past. "Don't worry. He's a smart kid."

"Sure, he's smart. I'm still going to worry. Everyone acts as if I'm being unreasonable and irrational. But you know better than anyone else that I'm *not*."

The words felt like a punch to the gut. They hadn't talked about this in years. He'd calmly tried to ignore the fact that her fears of her son learning to drive were entirely justified. Because of him.

"Jo," he said softly.

"I mean it. Someone I loved very much almost died in a car accident. When he was *sixteen*."

It killed him that he was still influencing her negative thoughts even now, years later. It was as if he'd painted on her youth with bold, broad brush strokes that were not entirely faded. Unfortunately, the picture was ugly. It was one of fear and abandonment. Pain. He'd done that to her.

And he'd never been able to fix it.

He tugged her into his arms. "He's Matt's son. He won't make my mistakes."

"Making Matt's mistakes wouldn't be much better."

"He'll make his own. We all do."

She bumped her head against his chest. "Look at me, with all the impressive small talk. I'm so boring. I'm the mother of a teenage boy who's about to get his driver's license. What am I even doing here?"

"You're here to dance and show everyone you're over that jackass. Now." Holding her hand, he walked her into the saloon.

The Silver Saddle was a classic honky-tonk owned by an Alabama native, Jimmy Hopkins and his wife, Trish. Like so many in their town, they were former military who'd found their second calling. The place was a classic throwback, with an often-broken-down mechanical bull in the corner they'd nicknamed Bertha. There were peanut shells on the floor. A stage was set up in the back where a live band played in front of a large dance floor perfect for line dancing. This was where Hud had discovered he'd actually liked country music. Or maybe what he'd really enjoyed was the challenge of learning the choreography of a line dance.

"Hiya, Hud," Jimmy said from behind the bar. "Hey there, Joanne. Long time."

Hud led them to the bar to fist-bump with Jimmy

and he ordered them both drinks. Jo took a seat on the bar stool next to him and took a pull of her beer.

Not two seconds later, Trish, Jimmy's wife, walked up to Jo and hugged her. "Oh my God, Joanne. I'm so *sorry*. Are you okay?"

"Yes, yes. I'm totally fine." She seemed to awkwardly accept the hug, patting Trish's back.

"Did you know Jimmy and I broke up a few weeks before our wedding day? Obviously, we got back together. Really, it was all my fault… By the way, I never liked Chuck anyway…" She went on and on, and after a bit Hud tuned her out.

He exchanged a look with Jimmy. After Joanne had assured Trish one thousand—or so it seemed—more times that she was doing well, thank you, Trish finally seemed to accept this. At that moment, the band began to play Tim McGraw's "A Real Good Man." The dance floor exploded with couples, and Hud tugged Jo on to the dance floor.

"Let's *show* Trish how well you're doing."

They fell into a natural rhythm on the dance floor as she kept in step with him. Jo smiled up at him, and he hoped her earlier worries were forgotten for now. Her hands came around his neck, announcing to everyone that tonight wasn't exactly business as usual for them.

Her hands were soft and warm. Despite the fact that he took pride in knowing how to two-step, he missed a step while staring at her full bottom lip. He recovered quickly, and pulled her closer, hands settling low on her waist. Then lower still.

Dancing might be mostly about form, but it also involved understanding your partner. It was about leading, but also sensing where she wanted to go and taking her there. Moving in time with the music. Recovering when you missed a step.

Hud had done that for most of his life, just not always on a dance floor.

She met his gaze, never missing her footing. Completely in time with his movements. Satisfaction spiked through him that this beautiful and wonderful woman was in his arms. He didn't deserve her.

The public nature of this night was new territory, but it also felt natural. Easy. Comfortable.

"Are you okay?" he asked, one hand drifting up and down her spine in a gentle caress.

He wanted to know that she was here tonight and in this relationship 100 percent. That there would be no regrets to jumping in full throttle with him. This relationship might seem quick to some but considering they'd been circling each other for over a decade, not so much. Not for him.

She was his. And he was hers, if she'd have him.

"I'm so good." She tilted her head and rose on tiptoes. "I'm claiming you, Hudson Decker. Tonight, you're mine."

"Always have been."

Heart slamming against his ribcage he took his

cue and bent to kiss her full on the lips in the middle of the crowded dance floor. As the song ended, he broke the kiss, conscious of the hush that had come over the room. But unable to break contact completely, he pressed his forehead to hers.

"If anyone has any questions about us now," Jo said, "they just haven't been paying attention."

He would have to agree.

Joanne strutted off the dance floor with Hud, trying to ignore the looks she received from some of the women in the room. They ranged from happily surprised, to envious, and dialed straight into angry ex-girlfriend territory. Well, too bad. They'd all had their chance with him and now it was her turn. Hud looked so good on the dance floor, moving with such practiced ease, holding her with confidence. When he'd swung her around in his capable hands, she'd entirely forgotten that she was the boring mother of a teenager and remembered that first and foremost she was a woman.

And the Tim McGraw song was perfect for Hud. He might be a "bad boy," but he was also a good man. A regular hero firefighter. A leader in the community. He'd come such a long way from the rebellious boy that wanted to drive fast cars and break a lot of hearts. They danced a few more songs, then headed back to the bar for another drink and this time when

Trish approached Joanne and pulled her to the side it was with zero pity in her eyes.

"Oh, girlfriend, way to bounce back! Hang on to that one."

Turning away from Trish, she spied Hud at the bar, casually reaching for his wallet from his back jeans pocket. He caught her eye as if he'd sensed she was looking, smirked and winked.

"Thanks. I better get back."

"Run."

She didn't run, not her, no sir, but she did rather quickly dash to his side. "I'm having so much fun. We should do this more often."

He waggled his eyebrows. "Yeah?"

The band had started another song, "Friends in Low Places," and it had become hard to hear above the music. "I said we should do this more often."

"I know," he said, or she thought he said. She wasn't all that skilled at reading lips.

Her skills lay elsewhere. Over the years she'd acquired a fair amount of skill at reading people and this was Hud, after all. She knew everything about him. Hud's heated looks and touches were telling her that he wanted her. He was almost making love to her on the dance floor with his hands, with his hot gazes. Hud was a red-blooded man who loved sex. Tonight, she was right there with him.

He was mid-pull on a beer when she reached as high as she could on her tiptoes and tugged him down to put her mouth near his ear. "I want to go home and have sex now!"

Hud looked as though he would spit out his beer in surprise, then he swallowed and grinned. "That's a pretty damn good offer."

She hoped so. Tonight, she wanted to show him that she'd learned her way around the bedroom, too. No wallflower, she knew how to please a man. She didn't think she'd ever felt this kind of longing and desire wrap around her. They'd been so close to being together again until they'd been interrupted. She didn't want to wait another day. Another hour.

"Let's go," he said, slammed his beer down and took her hand.

He followed her home in his truck. Jo observed the speed limit, thinking of her son, but found herself pushing it. As soon as she parked, Jo rushed up to the door to unlock it. Hud was right behind her, his arms wrapping around her waist from behind. She wiggled her butt into his crotch, hearing him groan.

"I'll get this door opened." The lock that stuck half the time was stuck again.

"Let me," he said, and took the key from her.

But they were both a little too distracted by each other and as he bent toward the lock, she licked his neck and kissed it, making him groan again. Then he took her in his arms, key and door forgotten, and kissed her, warm and wet and deep. She opened to him, giving him a preview of coming attractions as her tongue tangled with his. He pushed her up against the front door, pinning her there, and continued to shower her with openmouthed kisses. They were both breathing heavily when Hud stopped everything.

"What's wrong?"

"I… I can't believe I'm saying this, but—"

"But *what*?" Fear gripped her hard and wrapped around the back of her knees. He couldn't change his mind about them now. No, no, no. She was taking him to bed to have wild, hedonistic sex with him.

"I want to make you wait."

"Wait for *what*?"

He winced. "For us. To be together again."

"You said that with a straight face. Good job. That's funny. Okay, let's go inside." She turned to work on the lock again, but he whipped her around to face him.

"I mean it. I'm not having sex with you tonight." His words were not agreeing with his gaze, which looked pained.

"Hud, why not? Why are you doing this?" She pulled on his forearm. "This is what we both want."

"Because, Jo, I want to slow us down. I want to court you."

Court? Who even said that word anymore? "What are you talking about?"

"We jumped right in once before and that didn't work out so well. This time I want a change. And I need you to be sure. I keep telling you this is different for me, well, this is how I *show* you."

That was sweet, she had to admit. She still hated the idea. "Couldn't you find some other way of showing me?"

He pressed his forehead to hers. "Believe me, I've racked my brain. You're smarter than me. Come up with something. Anything. I'm begging you."

Damn, Hud was adorable when he begged. On the spot, she couldn't think of a single thing. He was right. Delaying the sex they both wanted to have and actually going out on dates to get to know each other was the opposite of what they'd done before.

"I think you're right," she said, miserably. "Waiting is the very opposite of our past. And we've waited this long…"

"What's another week or so?"

"*That* long?"

"Negotiable." He chuckled. "I could be talked out of a week."

"It's going to be my mission to talk you out of waiting that long." She pouted.

"Good night, Jo." He pulled away, almost prying her hand from his waist. "I'm calling you tomorrow."

"What's tomorrow?" She had work in the morning, and no idea what he had in mind.

"I'm calling to ask you out on a date." He took a couple of steps down.

"Yes."

"Yes, what?"

"I'll go out on a date with you. I'm just trying to save time here."

He smiled and her heart gave a powerful tug. "You are so damn cute."

"I think the word you meant is *sexy*." She did a shoulder shimmy.

His gaze darkened with heat. "That goes without saying."

"No, you *have* to say it. Often. I'm sexy."

"Noted."

He walked slowly toward his truck and she loved watching the way it seemed he fought with his own body to move each step. He didn't want to go. She loved that he didn't want to go but he was forcing himself to do it anyway. She stood feet planted on the porch, carefully watching him, hoping he'd have a change of heart. Knowing all the while that he wouldn't. Past history told her that when Hud made up his mind, nothing and no one could shake him.

In his truck, he rolled down the window. "Hey, sexy, I'm going to watch you walk inside."

She struggled with the key a little more and then it finally came unlocked. Opening it, she made a big show of walking in, then watched from the window as he drove away.

Joanne felt much better the following morning. Sexual frustration aside, she understood what Hud was trying to do. It made sense. After all, he knew better than anyone her six-month rule. She never slept with a guy before dating him exclusively for six months. After that, if all went well, another six months before a man was ever introduced to her son. Sue her if she'd done away with "the rules" for Hud. He was the exception, as he'd been around before she *made* the rules. She'd known him for far longer than six months and he'd known Hunter for his entire life.

But if he wanted to "court" her, she supposed she'd let him. He'd been very cute about it, after all.

"Still no word from the Taylors?" Joanne asked Nora later that morning at the shop.

"No, and this is getting rude."

"It passed rude a few days ago. Seems like they've found someone else." She hated the thought but had to consider it.

"They paid for your designs. That would be crazy and wasteful to hire someone else. Plus, they loved them."

"Maybe I'll have to pull out all the stops," Joanne said. "And fight for the business like I did once before. Start over. Pitch them another idea."

"There you go."

Joanne's phone buzzed with a text from Hud.

Picnic this afternoon.

Really? A picnic?

She texted back:

Who are you and what have you done with my best friend?

Hud: Meet me on Wildfire Ridge. I'm picking up a shift here today. Get Rachel from doggy day care and bring her. She'll love it too.

"Hud wants to take me on a picnic," Joanne said out loud.

"Aww," Nora said, clutching her chest.

"What's wrong with me that all I want to do is jump his bones?"

"There's nothing wrong with you. We are talking about Hud Decker, right? Hunk-a-licious."

"Shouldn't I be interested in more than sex, though? That's a little shallow of me."

"Not when you consider that you already know he's right for you in every way. He's your best friend and you know everything there is to know. All you need to know now is if you can move into that other, ahem, area, so who can blame you for wanting to fast-track it?"

Because of the only problem in this new and tenuous situation. Joanne wasn't sure that Hud was perfect for her in every way. Fun and carefree? Yes. Slightly dangerous in that oh-so alluring way? Uh-huh. But she'd been craving stability and security for so long in a relationship. She'd wanted something that would last. More children, without any possibility of being a single mom again.

Then again, she'd thought Chuck could give her that and it had all been a big, fat lie. She wondered why and how she'd convinced herself she could have security and a future with Chuck, of all people. She hated the first answer that came to mind, but she'd never thought that any other woman would want Chuck, so he was a safe bet. He also had a plan for his future and shared it often.

Later that afternoon, Joanne headed to pick up Rachel and drove up the hill to Wildfire Ridge. She loved this area and its stark and rugged beauty. Hud spent a lot of time here now, both as a part-time guide and head architect of the controlled burns. For years, they'd warded off another wildfire and the wildlife had slowly returned. Mountain lions and deer dotted the hill at times and didn't bother anyone as long as they were left alone. Of course, you really didn't want to have a little dog run loose deep in the hills, but Rachel would be on her leash and wouldn't stray up into the farthest parts of the ridge, where the mountain lions tended to roam.

"Okay, we're here."

Joanne still wore her work clothes, a wraparound red dress and matching flats, because she hadn't wanted to take time and go home and change. The September waning sun would set before long. They'd had a long summer, but soon autumn would arrive, her favorite time of the year even if it meant shorter days and longer nights. She'd just bet Hud could keep her warm all fall and winter long. And just like that her mind was in the gutter again. She couldn't wait to be in bed with him, cuddling, sharing heat, sharing… Everything.

Parking in the designated area, she climbed out, clipped the leash on Rachel and began walking up the trail to the hill. The ground was dusty after a long hot and dry summer but the trees, here for longer than the town, stood firm and tall. They'd weathered rain, drought, and fires with their deep roots. Wildflowers sprouted up here and there across the ridge, spreading a splash of color. Yellow and orange. Purple. The sky was a clear blue and the air smelled crisp and clean with hints of impending autumn. No wonder Hud loved it here.

Twigs snapped as she stepped over them. Wildfire Ridge Outdoor Adventures had been started by Jill, with activities for those Silicon Valley types seeking so-called extreme sports. They had guided hikes into mountain lion territory, wakeboarding and waterskiing on Anderson Lake, rock climbing and ziplining. Joanne had been here once, on Family and Friends day right before their opening and not since then.

She spied Hud in the distance dressed in the guides' uniform, tan cargo pants, boots and a matching long-sleeved black tee pushed up to his elbows.

He was speaking with a small group, possibly the one he'd taken on a guided hike. When he turned and caught her eye, he winked and then nudged his chin. And there a few feet in front of her and to the left under a tree was a blanket spread out with a cooler on top.

"Oh my gosh, he really meant a *picnic*."

Joanne set Rachel down on the blanket and snooped inside the cooler. She found cold beers and what appeared to be salad containers and sandwiches from her favorite deli in town. He'd even brought doggie snacks for Rachel.

"You're going to like this," she said, picking one out for Rachel. She'd been so good on the car ride, sitting on her haunches like a real person.

She turned to give it to Rachel, and… No Rachel.

The leash was gone, too, which meant she'd taken off. Cursing herself for not setting the leash under the heavy cooler, she stood and frantically turned in a circle. She couldn't see Rachel anywhere, and then out of the corner of her eye she saw a white blur. *Rachel!* Headed toward certain death, no doubt, if she got anywhere near mountain lion territory. But damn if Joanne would let that happen. Hud would never forgive her. Rachel was a cute dog with a ridiculous name who'd never hurt anyone.

Kicking off her flats, Joanne began to run in the direction she'd seen Rachel go.

Chapter Nine

Hud has just finished up with the group he'd guided through a seven-mile hike when he caught a blur of red flashing in his peripheral vision.

Jo was running—which she swore to him she'd never do unless someone was chasing her—screaming, "Raaaa-chellll!"

For someone who didn't run at all, she was moving quickly. But she didn't look particularly equipped to be running on the hill, dressed in a short red dress.

"Who's that?" One of the hikers asked.

"That's my…girlfriend. If you'll excuse me." He dropped his backpack and took off after Joanne, who he guessed had to be running after Rachel.

Here's what he'd learned recently as a dog owner: dogs are pack animals. The owner is the pack leader. They want nothing more than to please you, so teach them how. And finally, and he'd learned this one the hard way: never, ever, *chase* a dog if your intention is to catch him. They'll think it's a game. But apparently no one had given Jo the 411 and she thought she'd be able to catch Rachel, who not only outran Jo, but became a little airborne at times. Like a gazelle.

He ran after Jo, who ran after Rachel, who ran for the sake of running. Because she was a dog.

"Jo! Don't chase Rachel!" he yelled.

Jo didn't seem to hear him and with a solid lead, she was still several feet away from Hud. Headed toward the lake.

"No, Rachel! Noooooo!" Joanne waved her arms in the air. "Don't go in the laaaaake!"

In other relevant news, Rachel knew how to swim and rather liked it. Hud was gaining on Jo but just when he was almost close enough to touch her, she jumped in the lake after Rachel. Her dress swimming around her neck, she finally registered Hud's presence.

"Don't worry! I'll get her." She then began to swim after Rachel, who, Hud hated very much to tell Jo, was already drying herself off. On him. He picked her up.

"Jo," he said, biting back a laugh. "She's right here, babe."

She turned in a circle, caught him holding Rachel, then swam back to the edge of the lake. He held out his other hand to haul her out. Wet and muddy, she gave him a little smile. "Good. She's okay."

He pulled her into his arms. "C'mere."

She was shivering. "I thought I'd lost her forever."

He didn't think he'd ever loved Jo more than at this moment. She'd probably crawl under Mrs. Diaz's spider infested house for Rachel, too. Fearless. "She knows how to swim."

"I just found that out." She reached to pet Rachel. "Did you enjoy that little dip, princess?"

"More than you did." Hud chuckled.

"Are you *laughing* at me?"

"Not at all. I prefer to keep my family jewels intact, thanks." He continued to rub her back in small circles. "You're freezing."

She fisted her hands in his now-damp tee. "And I ruined our picnic."

"Nah. We'll just be relocating."

With that, he walked holding Jo's hand, carrying Rachel in the other. In his backpack, he found his SOL orange emergency blanket and tore it open to cover Jo with it.

"Thank you." She drew it tighter around her.

He walked her to his truck and went back to get the picnic blanket and cooler, putting everything, including his backpack, in the bed of his truck.

He hopped in the front seat. "We'll come back

for your car later. This way you won't get your car seat damp."

She pulled on his wrist. "I'm really sorry."

"Nothing to be sorry about. You were trying to save Rachel."

"Who didn't need saving." She sighed.

"Let me tell you a few things about dogs…"

He reiterated everything he'd learned since she encouraged him to adopt the rescue pet while he drove them back to his place. Foolishly, he hadn't prepared to have her over for company. But thanks to his time in the Army, he kept a clean house. Mostly. And also had a maid come in twice a week when he was gone on rotation. Besides, Jo had been over here many times before for a movie, or the few times they'd double-dated with other people. But okay, yeah, he usually prepped better than this.

He'd had every intention of taking her back to her home after the picnic and keeping his hands to himself once again. It was killing him, sure, but she was worth it. They were worth waiting for. He just knew it would be explosive between them because those kisses were simply a hint at what was to come. Given the change of plans this afternoon, he'd have his first real challenge. Because seeing her with that dress floating around her neck and the view below through the clear lake water had him nearly swallowing his tongue.

Inside, he encouraged her into a warm shower and gave her a towel and his bathrobe.

"I'll put your dress in the dryer." He stopped, re-thinking. "*Can* it be put in the dryer?"

She gazed at him from under hooded eyes. "Thank you for asking, but yes, it can."

With that, she removed the dress and wiggled out of black lace panties and a matching bra.

She smiled and tossed them to him. "So glad we're doing this whole waiting thing."

He swallowed hard. This idea to wait had seemed like a good one at the time.

While she was in the shower, he fed Rachel, then settled her in the kennel. He got busy arranging for a picnic on the living room floor. Okay, he was officially corny. If the guys at the station could see him now, they'd razz him until the end of time. He'd never been a fool like this over a woman. He didn't feel good about that now because maybe he'd been unfair to the women he'd dated in the past. While he'd tried to be clear about his intentions, he knew there were some ex-girlfriends who'd believed they'd be the one to change him. To get him to finally settle down.

One of them had sat here in this very living room on a double date with him, Jo and some loser she'd dated a couple of years ago. Not Chuck, but still not good enough. Jo had later warned him that Kristine had every intention of making herself "the one." Maybe his stance had made him a bit of a challenge to her, but he hadn't intended that. And when she'd kindly told him, after realizing they weren't going anywhere, that he should just go ahead and tell Jo he was madly in love with her, he'd made *Kristine* sound like the paranoid one.

"Don't be ridiculous," he'd said, or something equally inane.

She'd just smiled and told him to think about it, and to call and thank her when he finally figured it out for himself.

But up until now—what he considered his last chance, whenever he'd allowed himself to consider the possibility—he believed he still wasn't ready to give Jo everything she deserved. That he had to earn more money. Had to save more. Buy a bigger house with plenty of room for both Jo and Hunter to move in with him. Get rid of some of his workout equipment in his spare room to make space for her fabrics and dresses she liked to bring home. Those were all excuses, he now realized.

Because deep down he was terrified of losing her all over again. Deeper still in those small tight spaces where he didn't often dare to look, he wondered if he was the problem. Maybe she couldn't ever love him like she had the first time. Maybe gold didn't strike twice.

Jo emerged from the bathroom wearing his bathrobe, which pretty much swam on her, coming down to her ankles. Despite that, she looked like a cover girl model to him. Her blond hair was damp and pushed back behind her ears. She was fresh-faced, all the makeup washed off, making her appear even younger.

"That was just what I needed." She walked to the edge of the blanket he'd now laid in the middle of the living room. "Oh wow."

This time, he'd added a few touches he wouldn't have ever attempted on Wildfire Ridge. Candlelight. Plates and actual flatware instead of the plastic stuff.

"Ready for our picnic?" Crouching, he dished out her favorite salad on a plate.

She sat on the blanket, then opened up the robe so that her legs were showing. "How did I never know that you're this romantic?

"Probably because I'm not."

"Hud, this—" she waved her hand over the area "—is romantic."

"I'm trying."

"And I love that you're trying." She scooted closer to him, giving him a good whiff of his own soap. On her.

That hint of intimacy drove him wild. He tucked her in close. "You deserve it."

"It's funny you should say that, because I gave up on this kind of thing a while ago. Expectations."

He let that statement settle in his bones, realizing that he'd done something for her no other guy had. "Why?"

She shrugged. "When I became a mom, I gave up on romance and shucked it for responsibility. Security."

"You can have both, you know."

"You're reminding me of that."

They ate quietly for a few minutes, he nearly inhaling his sandwich, rethinking this whole "waiting" thing. How long had they known each other, anyway? Even if their relationship had recently changed status, he'd waited long enough for her. She was finally available, and he'd made his move. He'd made it clear she was special, and not one of his many seductions. Sure, it would be better to know that she was truly over the idiot and not just distracting herself with Hud. Because he needed her whole body and mind and wasn't going to accept anything less.

When Jo crawled into his lap, she had unbelted the robe, and beautiful fleshy soft skin brushed up against him.

"Can I talk you out of waiting? I mean, I nearly died trying to save Rachel."

"I have a feeling you could talk me into anything."

Her fingers threaded through his hair, and he began to lose focus on anything other than her mouth. "I want you so much. Tonight."

"And I need you to be sure." Parting the robe, his hand explored under it, tweaking her nipple.

She moaned. "I'm sure. I've never been more certain of anything in my life."

With that assurance, Hud put out the candlelight, drew her into his arms and stood, carrying her toward the bedroom.

Flush with anticipation, Jo held tight to Hud's shoulders as he carried her. The wait was over. She would undress him and get to witness up close and personal all of that gorgeous taut skin and muscle. With Hud, she easily lost any inhibitions because tonight he'd made her feel desired and special. He'd proved something to her, and now it was her turn to do the same. To let him know he wasn't any rebound guy. He was Hud. *Her* Hud. Always had been, and always would be. No matter what.

Did she think this meant forever? No. She was a grown-up now.

After their very first time, she'd made big plans. Plans to get married, since of course they would have had to now they'd had *sex*. But she wasn't that young and idealistic girl anymore. Life didn't go according to plan. And this time she wasn't going to pin Hud down to anything permanent. Better to take it one day at a time and see where it went. Along the way, she was going to enjoy every second because she'd been holding back for too long.

Hud laid her gently on his bed, and she wiggled out of the robe and tossed it aside. She let herself drink in the sight of his heated gaze, taking in the view.

"What are you waiting for?" She stretched her arms out, wiggling her fingers for him to come and join her.

"We're not waiting," he said, slow and rough as he pulled off his shirt with one hand.

Coming up on her knees beside him, she went for his pants, unsnapping and sliding them down his slim hips. Then, finally, his boxer briefs came off and she thought she'd never seen anything more beautiful. Hud was all man, sharp angles and planes. Hard everywhere. She ran the pads of her fingers down his chest to his abs and luxuriated in each sinewy muscle, and the sensations as he tensed beneath her touch.

"I want to touch you everywhere."

"I'm not going to stop you."

His big hand covered her butt while his mouth came down eagerly to her nipple, sucking hard. Her body buzzed with a sweet ache, and warmth spread between her thighs. Still standing beside her on the bed, hand on the nape of her neck, he tugged her mouth to his for a long deep kiss. Then he took them both down to the bed, his hard body covering hers. She wrapped her legs around his back, burying her face in his warm neck. Licking. Tasting.

"I missed this." She'd never felt this physically connected to anyone else. Her body purred and vibrated under his touch. "I missed *you*."

"We're going to take our time." Hud braced himself above her with a slow smile. "You don't have to be anywhere for the next twenty-four hours, do you?"

He didn't wait for her answer, as he slowly crawled down her body, kissing and licking as he went. His tongue played with the shell of her ear and when his teeth sank into her earlobe, a wild and unexpected pull of desire made her thighs throb and pulse. His lips nibbled at her nipples and sucked each one until she bucked under him, opening her legs.

"Patience."

He kissed and licked his way down, playing with her belly button. But when he lowered his head between her thighs, far from patient, Joanne became so aroused her hips gyrated and her legs trembled. She fought the cresting wave and tried to regain control as he pushed her higher. The wave came anyway, and with one more lick from him in just the right spot, she lost all control. She moaned his name, suddenly aware that she had her hands in his hair, clutching him tight.

"Oh, Hud. I'm sorry." Letting go, she smoothed his hair down from the tufts she'd created. Good thing he had a lot of hair. "I hurt you."

He braced above her, looking no worse for the wear. "I didn't feel a thing."

She quirked a brow though she knew exactly what he meant.

"I didn't feel a thing on my head." He gave her a wicked smile. "The big one."

"C'mere." She pushed him until he went flat on his back. Naturally, he went willingly.

She could feel his body tense as she lowered herself over him, licking down his flat abs, and then licking down to the promised land. She licked once, twice, and took him into her mouth. He groaned and his muscles tensed to the consistency of granite as she teased him mercilessly until he was at the edge of where she wanted him.

When he'd finally had enough, he made her stop and rolled on top of her. "Condom."

Yes, finally!

He rustled through his nightstand to where she assumed he kept his stash of condoms. She wouldn't know. And she didn't much want to think about that right now. The stash of ready condoms. She'd prefer he had only a couple in there, specifically for *her*, maybe even with her name on them, were she wishing for a miracle.

"Shit," he said. "I'm out."

While she wondered just how much sex he'd been having lately to be completely out, he added, "I haven't bought any in a while. It's been…a long time."

Joanne tried not to let that bit of information get to her, but damn if it did.

Her playboy best friend, condom-less.

With her.

"And we were going to wait," he added.

This would all be incredibly upsetting if Joanne wasn't prepared. She'd learned her lesson the hard way, after all. *Never* depend on a man to bring the birth control. Hud looked absolutely disgusted with himself, poor baby.

Joanne bent over the bed to reach for her purse and brought out a tiny silver foil packet. "I'm not out."

Hud brightened, even more so when Joanne ripped the package open and slid the condom on his shaft. She stroked him once, then twice, making him groan. Taking over, he braced himself on top of her. He kissed her, warm and deep making her skin tingle all over, and in one deep thrust he was inside her, making them both gasp.

She'd never seen anything as beautiful as Hud's face, a mask of concentration as he moved inside of her, deeper and harder each time. He wasn't the boy she'd loved once beyond all reason, but a man. A grown man, who'd been through so much and yet he'd never left her behind. He'd always come back to her, one way or another. The knowledge of that pierced her, and she let go of a little more control, allowing the sensations to roll and sway through her body.

The pressure built inside her quickly, like nothing she'd experienced before. She and Hud were like fire together, explosive, both urging each other to the pinnacle in soft whispers and ragged breaths. She bucked against him, wanting more, wanting deeper, harder, and he gave it to her. Faster and deeper he went, taking her higher, until she fell apart in a sweet climax. Only then did he let go and had his own release.

"We've gotten a lot better at that," Joanne said on a ragged breath. She was including herself in there, though it was mostly Hud, were she being completely honest.

Hud tucked her to his side. "I didn't have a whole lot to offer you then, other than my enthusiasm."

"You definitely had that in spades. But you were also very sweet."

"Sweet? Me?"

"Yes, *you*. Or I probably wouldn't have fallen in love with you."

They were both too quiet for a moment, as if the raw memory had shattered them both a little.

"Stay with me tonight," he said, brushing a kiss against her knuckles. "Sleep with me."

"Will I actually get any sleep?"

"We can do some of that, if you want."

"Okay," she said, snuggling closer. "But you have to promise me something. It's very important."

"Anything."

"Next time I take a shower, don't leave me in there alone."

Chapter Ten

"Is it a beautiful day, or is it just me?" Joanne set her coffee orders down. "One soy latte for me, one caramel macchiato for you."

Joanne's good mood wouldn't quit. She had Hud to thank for that.

"It's supposed to be in the eighties later today," Nora grumbled. "I wish fall would hurry up and get here already. You know that's when my order will change to pumpkin spice latte, right?"

"Sure, that's when everything changes to pumpkin spice."

Nora wrinkled her nose. "And you hate pumpkin, so why do you sound so happy about that?"

"I'm not happy about that." Joanne took another swallow of her now-lukewarm latte.

"What's got you in such a good mood?" Nora studied her intently for several seconds. "Oh my gosh, you got laid, didn't you?"

Was she *that* obvious? "What makes you say that?"

"You look the most relaxed you've been in weeks. No, wait. Months."

Joanne supposed there was nothing quite like multiple orgasms to put a little spring in her step, but she hadn't imagined it would be written all over her face. Still, she wasn't going to talk about it. In detail. She was old-fashioned that way.

"Okay, me and Hud. No more waiting."

Nora smiled and threw a hand over her mouth in mock surprise. "Oh, color me shocked!"

Joanne snorted. "You are *not*."

"No, I'm not, because I called it."

"I ruined our picnic and we wound up back at his place." Joanne explained the failed picnic, her impromptu swim in the lake, and later the resulting amazing picnic save on the living room floor.

"Holy cow, this dude is so romantic. I had no clue. But when you think about it, suddenly all the sweet things he's done for you over the years take on a different perspective. Like the Bahamas thing. And also, that time Chuck forgot your birthday, and you later found out it was Hud who sent you those red roses and candies."

She'd almost forgotten about that. He was also the only one besides her mother who remembered the anniversary of her father's death and came over to dispense hugs, go with her to the cemetery and listen to her cry. Over the years, there had been so many sweet gestures that she'd attributed solely to their best friend status.

They got to work together on Jill's alterations, on their knees hemming the dress by hand, chatting the entire morning. When the door chimed, Nora went to the front of the shop to see whether it was the UPS guy or the mailman. A few seconds later, she returned, face frozen.

Bad news. Oh no, *bad news*.

Joanne stood. "What is it? Is it Hunter? Is he okay?"

"It's not Hunter and no one is hurt." She hooked her thumb toward the front of the shop. "But you're probably going to have to deal with Chuck."

Chuck. "He's here?"

Why in God's name was he here? She assumed it wasn't to pay for his half of the wedding but speaking of that… Joanne rushed to the front of the shop.

There he stood, hands in his pockets, avoiding eye contact.

"I'm so glad you're here," Joanne said through

gritted teeth. "You ran out on me without paying for your half of the wedding."

"I'm sorry. Chuck was so confused. He didn't know what to do."

And there went the dreaded third person crap again. "Confused? About what? Directions to the venue? Date? Time? Really, what was so confusing, *Chuck*?"

"You. You confused me. We agreed to get married, but I knew you didn't really love me."

"Wow, okay, what a cop-out. And if you didn't think I loved you, could you have possibly mentioned that to me *before* the wedding day?"

"I know my timing sucked. Chuck isn't known for his timing." He shrugged.

Joanne's hands curled into fists. "Stop talking about yourself in the third person! It's not cute. It's just…weird."

"You used to think it was funny."

"I used to think a lot of things. Like what a good husband you'd make. Boy, was I delusional."

"Exactly. Delusional."

"You don't get to call me delusional!" She pointed to her chest. "Only I get to call myself delusional."

"Okay, okay. I'm sorry! But did you ever stop to think what it was like for me to know you'd have preferred Hud over me in a heartbeat? But he wasn't 'husband material.'" He held up air quotes. "He's a playboy. Well maybe I didn't want to be second best.

You're delu—kidding yourself if you don't realize you're in love with Hud."

"Oh, there you go again with all the paranoid jealousy. Hud has just always been there for me, unlike some people."

"And he loves you and you love him. I was always the third wheel when it came to you two. Private jokes, all the playful teasing. C'mon! Get real."

"I'm sure this is all your way of calling attention away from yourself. I'm not the one who was apparently cheating. I heard about your new girlfriend."

He tossed up his hands. "Hey, I didn't start things up with her until I knew it was over between us."

"Great. That must have been, what, on our wedding day or the day before?" She forced some calm into her voice and went to dig in her purse. "Lucky for you, I prepared you a bill for the wedding. I was going to ask you for half, but now I think you had better pay me for the whole thing."

He cleared his throat. "I'm actually here, not just to apologize…but to get my mother's wedding ring back. I want to give it to Mandy."

Damn him. He'd come here for the ring. Not to sincerely apologize. Not because he was remorseful for what he'd done. No. He needed something from her.

The stupid, awful ring.

On the day of her wedding fail, Joanne had tossed that family heirloom into the trash, but Hud had taken it back out, saying it might be worth something. She could pawn it and get some money for Chuck's half of the wedding. It might have been a good idea, but the ring wasn't worth much other than sentimental value. She'd had it appraised before the wedding to see if she should insure it.

"I don't have it," Joanne said, and that was the truth. She'd thrown it in the bottom of her underwear drawer, unwilling to look at it even among the rest of her jewelry.

"Did you *pawn* it?" Chuck had the nerve to look disgusted.

"I should have, but no, I didn't." She crossed her arms, an evil thought forming. "What's it worth to you?"

"It was my *mother's* ring. You know the right thing to do is just give it back to Chuck. Chuck is supposed to give it to his wife and obviously you're not going to be his wife. Anymore."

Ah, how had she never noticed that before? Chuck used the third person whenever he said something awkward. Uncomfortable. To distance himself, maybe.

Like when he'd said: Chuck loves Joanne.

"Well, Chuck is a *crazy* person if he thinks I'm going to give him back the ring without getting him to pay his fair share of the wedding."

"Be reasonable. I just got through two rounds of the draft and I've no idea when or if I'll get officially drafted to the majors and start earning some real money."

"Dive into your savings."

"*What* savings?"

"All the money you said you were slowly putting aside for our future!"

"Oh, that." He shrugged. "I just said that so you'd think I was a better bet than Hud."

Joanne's stomach churned with what had to be volcano lava. She saw a red haze appear in front of Chuck. He was glowing. Yes, yes. She was going to kill him. The bill she'd been holding was crunched up in her fist.

"You liar! You're never getting the ring back! Never!" Joanne flung herself at him, ready to punch him in the throat, but Nora had obviously heard, come running and pulled Joanne back by the waist.

"Don't. He's not worth it."

Recoiling, Chuck headed for the door and then turned one last time. "This isn't over. I need that ring and I'll get it, one way or another."

"Get out of here!" Nora screamed. "I can't hold her back much longer. She's going to blow!"

Chuck left like the coward that he was, and it took everything in Joanne not to chase him down the street screaming, "Liar, liar, pants on fire!"

But that probably wouldn't be good for business.

"Breathe. In and out. In and out," Nora said, finally letting go of Joanne.

Joanne staggered to the couch in front of the pedestal where prospective brides tried on their dresses. Anger coursed through her, making her skin prickly. Chuck had lied to her. He'd pretended to be someone he was not. Why? Then another realization hit her and when it did, hard and fast, she felt gut punched.

"Oh my God, he's right."

Chuck was the consolation prize. She'd never wanted anyone other than Hud.

"About the ring? No. It may be a family heirloom but holding it hostage is how you get to him to pay for the wedding. That's smart and fair."

Joanne's breaths were coming short and sparse. A cold shiver spiked down her spine. She'd wasted years chasing security and stability when she'd really wanted Hud. But he'd been so unavailable, and so… So risky. What kind of a terrible person traded true love for security?

The kind who wants more children but swore she'll never be a single mother again.

The kind who's a bit of a coward when it comes to her heart.

Nora appeared with a glass of cold water. "Here, hon."

"I'm a horrible person," Joanne said, accepting the glass.

"Don't say that. Everybody makes mistakes."

"Not everybody gets engaged to a…a man like Chuck because she wants the security and safety of having someone who she believes will always stick around."

"You're not being fair to yourself. Most women want that in a man."

"Not enough to give up on love."

"*Did* you? Give up on love?"

"I didn't think so," Joanne said. "But the humiliation of being stood up caused me the most pain. Being dumped for someone younger was hurtful, too. But I haven't really missed Chuck...at all."

Whenever she fought with Hud, and they didn't talk for a few days, she was gutted. Lost.

"I guess that tells you something," Nora said.

It told her that she still loved Hud Decker, her polar opposite. A man who'd never been risk averse. He'd driven too fast and crashed his car at sixteen in a horrible accident. He'd enlisted in the Army. He worked in a high-risk profession and loved extreme sports. He rode a motorcycle.

Hud Decker was the opposite of safety and security.

And still, all she wanted to do was text Hud everything that had just happened. But she'd have him come over instead. She wanted a hug from her best friend, the ones that cured everything.

Probie J.P. had a lot to learn. The first twenty-four of Hud's shift had been relatively calm. Only a few medical calls and then some drills he made the crew go through. The next morning their crew had been sitting at the breakfast table enjoying Alex's Belgian waffles, when J.P. said the worst thing a firefighter could ever say:

"I hope it's not quiet today."

"Rookie, never say that again," Hud said through gritted teeth. "Keep in mind when you say that you're wishing harm on others."

Every first responder possessed a strong superstitious streak. Utter those few words and the day was guaranteed to be utter chaos. And it was. Thanks to J.P., they were called out to assist at a two-alarm fire at a warehouse in San Jose. Several hours later that was under control when they were called back to Fortune to a brush fire by the freeway which had spread quickly. They stopped rush hour traffic to put it out and then everyone was miserable.

But beyond J.P.'s ignorance about firehouse superstitions, there was an underlying disregard for orders. And if Hud didn't rein him in quickly, this would not end well. Near the end of the day, Hud called J.P. into his office to have a little chat.

Hud shut the door.

"Am I in trouble?" J.P. asked.

Arms crossed, Hud leaned back against his desk. "I'll put it this way—you're skating. Next time I give you an order, I expect you to obey it to the letter or you're out on your ass. No questions asked. You're on probation and I can't afford you to get hurt out there."

"I'm sorry, I'm just anxious to get out there. Make a difference, you know?"

"I get it, but you can't get ahead of the learning curve for this job."

Hud might take risks but he was now calculated about them. No matter what he attempted, he always had an exit strategy. Always. He'd learned the hard way that not all risks were worth taking. Now, to impart this heady wisdom to a rangy twenty-two-year-old, who reminded Hud of himself at that age. In other words, J.P. believed he had balls of steel and that nothing could touch him. Ten years ago, Hud had been in the Army at twenty-two and stationed in North Carolina. Far from home, he'd learned to depend on himself and his unit. They grew as close as brothers, which was how he felt about the men in his firehouse.

"We're a family here," Hud said. "And that means we look out for each other. Think of me as your older brother. You can count on me to set you straight when you're screwing up."

"Okay, good."

Hud bent until he was nearly nose to nose with J.P. "You're screwing up, J.P."

Close to thirty minutes later, Hud felt that he'd put enough of the fear of God into J.P. and let him go with one last warning. As he got ready to update the LT coming on duty for the next forty-eight, his phone buzzed.

Jo: I need you tonight.

He smiled. Oh *yeah*. Round two. He texted back:

Shift ends at seven. I'll be over with dinner.

After a night like the one they'd had, he'd had a difficult time thinking of anything besides Jo. On his quiet day, when they'd been sitting around making bets on the 49er game, his thoughts had run to Jo. The sweet little sounds she made when he kissed the right spot. Her energy and passion to go all night with him. He just wanted more of the same, over and over.

He'd waited so long for this chance. Biding his time—for what? To be perfect? There was no such thing. But Jo made plans and she liked order in her life. Now more than ever he understood that need. She wanted stability and security and he didn't blame her for that. After what she'd been through, it was only natural. For the first time in his life, Hud thought he could give that to her. He was ready.

He picked Rachel up and then Chinese food from their favorite place in town. When Jo met him at the door wearing a very short halter dress, it took everything in him not to push her up against the wall and forget the food. Instead, he set Rachel down where she went trotting inside like she owned the place.

"Hey," she said, the corners of her sweet mouth pulling down. "I need a hug."

He set the cartons of food down on the kitchen table and tugged her into his arms. His hand slid up and down her back. "What is it? More bad luck boutique?"

"No. *Chuck* came by today."

Hud's heart nearly stopped and everything inside of him went still and cold. He didn't think Chuck would have the balls to show up again. There had to be a damn good reason he would risk the fear of Hud's wrath for that.

"What did he want?"

"Get this. He wants the ring he gave me, so he can give it to his new fiancée."

Good thing he'd fished that out of the trash. Jo hadn't been thinking straight. "Good. Give it back to him."

She pulled out of his arms to look for plates and set them down on the table. "Not until he pays me back what he owes me."

"Right. When will he have it for you?" He opened cartons and they fell into a natural rhythm. After all, they'd had dinners like this many times before.

"He *lied* about the money he was setting aside for our future. He has no savings, or so he claims. No way he can pay me back. That's why I'm holding his ring hostage."

Chuck was becoming a bigger jerk than Hud

thought possible. No savings. Jackass. How had he planned on helping Jo? Contributing? Hud had been saving for years, not that he'd mentioned that to her.

"Just hock it."

"The only value this ring has is sentimental. I had it appraised and it's not worth much."

"You think he'll somehow find the money to pay you back?" Hud doubted this, and he was also beginning to resent the idea of Jo keeping that ring.

It might be stupid, but he considered that holding on to that ring could be a symbol of not moving on.

Jo served each of them some chow mein and broccoli beef on their plates, then sat down across from him. "I don't think he'll be motivated any other way. Do you?"

Hud considered this, but his own desires were getting in the way of Jo's reasoning. He had to put them aside and think logically. "Do you have the money to pay for the wedding yourself?"

"Yes, because I saved, but it's the principle of the thing."

"I think you should give him back the ring."

Jo dropped her fork and it made a shrill clank. "Are you serious? Why? He's never going to pay me a dime otherwise."

"He may never pay you back anyway. In the meantime, you have his mother's ring."

"But it's my only insurance."

"Insurance for the money, or insurance he'll continue to have to deal with you? Maybe you're holding on and not letting go."

"I have moved on, buddy." She stood and pointed in the direction of her bedroom. "You and me, we moved on. Have you forgotten?"

"Never."

"I wouldn't be *with* you if I hadn't moved on."

"Then give him back the ring and make it official."

She made a frustrated sound. "Why are you being so unreasonable about this? I've got something he wants, so he's going to have to give me what I want."

"Okay, Jo. Do it your way. I'd just rather have him out of your life once and for all."

"And so would I," Jo said, coming around to his chair, straddling him. "But I have to do this my way. Don't be mad?"

When her fingers threaded through his hair, he lost focus entirely. Ring or not, *he* had Jo. As far as Hud was concerned, that was the real prize. And if Chuck ever wanted Jo back, he'd have a hell of a fight on his hands.

Hud guaranteed it.

"I can never stay mad at you, babe." When she buried her face in his neck and kissed, then licked, he forgot how hungry he was, too. He stood with her still straddling his hips. "Let's go."

She giggled. "What about dinner?"

"Later."

Chapter Eleven

Three days later, Joanne waited at the boutique for a scheduled appointment with a prospective bride when the phone rang.

"Joanne's, how can I help you?"

"It's Patricia Taylor."

Finally, they'd decided to return her calls. "We never settled on a dress from the designs you paid for and I'd hoped to get started on the dress soon."

"That's the thing. Would you please go ahead and send the designs over to Trudy's Boutique in San Francisco? We've decided to have them make the dress."

Trudy's was by far Joanne's biggest competition,

an exclusive boutique only the most privileged of brides could afford.

She forced her voice into professional mode and out of the whine she heard in her head. "Did we do anything wrong? I thought you had agreed to keep your business in Fortune."

The Taylors were from Fortune, originally from real estate entrepreneurs who were very public about supporting small businesses in Fortune. The deal had started out with such promise a few months ago, their enthusiasm for working with a local bridal boutique and an exclusively designed dress palpable.

Now everything was falling apart.

"I'm sorry, but we've decided to go with Trudy's. Your designs were by far the best ones and we'll go with one of those. You'll get credit for the design, of course."

But she wouldn't be making the dress, and Joanne knew how it would go. Her name might appear in the fine print, but it would essentially be buried. Trudy's would get all the publicity. Trudy's would be there on the day of the wedding for any last-minute alterations.

"Does this have anything to do with what happened recently? Because I can assure you, it's the best thing to have ever happened to me. I'm happier than I've ever been."

"I was so sorry to hear about that. Did the groom leave you hanging with all the expenses?"

"Well, yes. I'm handling it." Best not to go into the gory details with a client. "But the shop is in good standing and I wouldn't have any problems delivering the dress."

She cleared her throat. "I know you wouldn't. But the decision has been made. And Joanne, I would so appreciate it if you wouldn't spread the word that we're going to San Francisco for the dress. You know that our image is so closely tied with supporting local business. And we try to, in every instance possible."

Except this one.

"I'm a professional and not a gossip, but don't expect me to lie for you. We had an agreement and I'm willing and able to hold up my end."

"I just…you have to understand."

"Maybe if you explained." Joanne kept her words measured and even, leaving the emotion out of it.

"It might not be fair, but everything has to go perfect for my daughter's wedding. My husband expects it. He's not footing a six-figure wedding for something to go wrong with the dress."

"Is there some reason you believe I can't do the work?"

"Dear, you were just jilted!"

"It's not contagious, Patricia." Quoting Hud to a prospective client. New territory.

"That's not what I mean. You're normally so detailed oriented. But with everything you've been through, which was so unfair by the way, I don't have the same confidence in you." She took a breath. "I'm sorry."

"I'll put those designs in the mail for you. And best of luck." Joanne spoke sharply and hung up, her stomach churning.

She didn't think she'd ever sold a design without sewing the dress. Nothing like the feeling that a client didn't want Joanne to *touch* her dress to make her feel toxic. Her designs were good enough, apparently her hands were not. More than likely, her shop didn't have the sophisticated cachet of a big city boutique. Plus, there was the whole jilted bride bad luck boutique thing. The feeling of being passed over sank her spirits. Great that they were using her designs, but terrible that they didn't trust her enough to create them.

She wondered if that's how Hud felt about the ring. If he thought that she was keeping it because she didn't trust they would work out, so she had to hang on to some part of Chuck. To keep contact. But nothing could be further from the truth. She wanted Chuck out of her life. Maybe it was time to think about giving him the ring back like Hud wanted her to do. She didn't like the idea of giving Hud any doubts.

She gathered the designs from the back and slipped them into a manila envelope, addressing them to the Taylors of Fortune. They would be taking their business to San Francisco.

The doorbell jingled and a soft voice called out, "Am I too early?"

Joanne dashed to the front to meet her appointment, Leah Jones. "I'm sorry. I was in the back. My colleague has the day off."

Joanne led Leah to the couch and smiled. "Is there anyone else coming?"

Normally a bride brought in a mother or mother-in-law, best friend, or someone with her. Joanne or Nora would serve champagne as they looked at possible designs and talked wedding details, but this girl didn't look old enough to drink.

"No, it's just me. I'm not from the area."

Leah had long dark hair and wore little makeup. She wore faded jeans and a blue sweatshirt and definitely didn't look like Joanne's typical clients. She was slender. *Young.* Joanne decided against offering the champagne. Still, this was her favorite part of her work. Finding the love story that lived in each bride. Encouraging them to share the romance with her so that she could better come up with ideas for the perfect dress. Each bride then had a uniquely designed dress coming out of their own love story.

"Please, let's have a seat and discuss some ideas." Joanne waved her hand toward the couch and sat.

"Right off, I have to tell you that I don't have much money." Leah clutched her purse.

"Okay. I have several wedding budgets I can work with."

"I've saved up for this. It's going to be the most important part of my wedding day. I want a special dress that no one else has."

"Right. Well, that's what we do here." Joanne took out her sketch pad. "How old are you, Leah?"

"I look younger than I am," she said. "I'm twenty-one."

Old enough to drink alcohol. Joanne still wasn't going to break out the champagne. Leah was alone which meant she'd probably driven herself here. "How long have you known your groom?"

"I've known Jake since we were kids."

"And is he around? Will I get to meet him?"

"He'll be here for the wedding. His family is from Fortune. He already has approval for leave."

Another military man. "What branch?"

"Navy." She sat up straighter when she said so.

"Let me explain my process. What I do, initially, is listen to your love story. Then I come up with ideas once I get to know you. Tell me about you and Jake."

Leah relaxed, and her gaze took on that dreamy quality that Joanne loved so much. Too bad she hadn't noticed it had been missing in her. If she had, that might have been a clue that Chuck was all wrong for her. There was no love story there.

"We met when he was visiting his grandparents in Oregon, where I'm from. When he told me he was joining the Navy, I said I'd never speak to him again if he did."

Joanne gaped. "I'm s-sorry?"

"I know that sounds crazy." She giggled.

Joanne shook her head. No, it didn't sound crazy at all. It was almost exactly what she'd said to Hud when he signed up for the Army. He was eighteen, straight out of high school. After his car accident, he'd developed a kinship with first responders and knew it was what he wanted to do. Joanne was also eighteen, raising a one-year-old, still living at home and enrolled at junior college. The war was raging in the Middle East, and though Joanne was as patriotic as the next person, when someone she loved was shipping off it was a different story.

She hadn't wanted to lose him, even then. And she'd given him an ultimatum, as a best friend. If he went, he'd lose her friendship forever. He'd just smiled and said he was going anyway, hoped she'd change her mind, and he'd look her up when he got back.

If he got back.

For the second time in her life, Joanne had determined that loving Hud was too risky. But when he'd returned, they'd taken up as friends again just as if nothing had happened. Friendship had been safer when it came to him.

"Tell me more," Joanne said, ideas already coming.

"Well, of course, I was lying about the never talking to him again thing. I did talk to him again because thank God he came back. And after that we had this long-distance kind of thing. When I came out to visit him where he was stationed in Virginia, we got married."

"Oh, so you're already married?" It happened. Sometimes a bride wanted a second chance at the day of their dreams.

She held up her finger to indicate her story wasn't complete. "Then we got divorced, because living apart when you're married can be a real strain on a relationship."

"No kidding. This is a second wedding kind of thing?" And they were only twenty-one!

"Yes. This is the one where the entire family, both sides, are on board and they realize no one can talk us out of it." She smiled shyly. "He's my person."

"Your love story is very romantic. How do you feel about tulle?" Joanne went on, trying to capture a sense of what would appeal to Leah and would flatter her slender frame, dark hair and eyes.

"I want my dress to be blue," Leah blurted out. "Can you do that?"

"I can do anything you'd like," Joanne said. "Sure, blue isn't traditional but that's why you're here, right? You want something unique."

"Blue is my favorite color and he'll be dressed in his Navy dress blues. I want us to match."

To date, Joanne had only worked with one unconventional bride, Jill Davis. The first designs had involved something much like a swimsuit because Jill thought she and Sam would get married while wakeboarding. But when the mother of the bride had torpedoed that idea, Jill surprisingly went fairly conventional.

"Sweetheart neckline? Plunging back?" Joanne continued to ask questions to get a feel from Leah. "Pearl sequins?"

They continued to chat about possibilities, and Leah's eyes lit up with excitement.

A lot of people had asked Joanne why she hadn't designed her own wedding dress. She hadn't had the answer to that question, as it had once been her dream to design her wedding dress and sew it. She'd had in mind exactly what it would be. A sweetheart collar with a shorter train and a tiara. Individual pearls sewn on the bodice. A mix of traditional with a little whimsy. The short story? She'd settled. Time got away from her between work, readjusting to Matt being back in Hunter's life and Hunter's general "teenage" passage. And the Valentino dress had been such a steal with her discount. She'd chosen it even though Nora had said the long, Princess Diana-like train didn't say "Joanne." And she'd been right, of course.

Instead the dress said, "I'm thirty-two and I need to get on with it." Now the Valentino dress would probably be sold because Joanne would never jinx herself with it again. Or any other bride, for that matter. Maybe Tilly was right, and Joanne should burn it.

Joanne accepted half of the deposit that she normally asked for a design for the bride because Leah didn't have enough. Joanne would make it work. She had to, for a bride that had renewed Joanne's own hopes in love and romance, even at her age.

After her appointment, Joanne closed up the boutique and drove to her mother's home on the outskirts of Fortune. Mom had been bugging her to come by for days and Joanne had a feeling that it was due to the way rumors spread in their little town. By now Mom would have heard about Hud. And who knew what people were saying?

Looks like Hunky Hud is now having a fling with his best friend. In-te-res-ting.

Did you hear? Joanne's on the rebound with the hottest LT in town.

Sorry. Chuck who?

Her mother greeted Joanne at the door. "Sweetheart! Finally. I've been so worried."

"Sorry. I've just been so busy with the shop… and…" Hud. Busy getting busy with Hud. "Everything. You know how it is."

Mom led her into the cozy living room filled with photos and mementos of Joanne's childhood. Ramona Brandt did not believe in redecorating but instead kept a virtual museum of Joanne's past. There were photos of her and Dad everywhere, the man who, for most of her life, had been Joanne's hero. Tall, handsome and larger than life, he'd worked out regularly but still died of a massive stroke at his engineer's desk in Silicon Valley. High blood pressure, undiagnosed. He'd been too busy to see the doctor.

Not for the first time in her life, Joanne had felt abandoned by a man even if it wasn't entirely his fault. However, from that day on, she'd been obsessed with staying healthy. And sure, maybe a little bit preoccupied with safety and security. Who could blame her?

"Want some coffee?" Mom asked.

"You know I can't drink coffee this late or I'll be up all night."

"Decaf?"

"Okay. Sure."

Joanne waited for her mother to come back from the kitchen, scrolling through her phone to avoid the photos of her smiling dad looking down on her. From heaven, if you believed in that sort of thing, and Joanne did. What would he think about the mess she'd made out of her life? He'd always encouraged her to take risks. To try out for the volleyball team even if she was at best an average player. To apply for the school of her dreams. To ask out the boy she was interested in, instead of waiting for him to ask her.

But at some point, Joanne had chosen safety over happiness.

Mom brought in the cups and set them on the table

near the leather couch, which had seen better days. "Have you read the book yet?"

"What book?"

She cocked her head. "The grief book."

Oh yeah. That. No. She hadn't. "I'm not going to read that book."

"Why not?"

"Because nobody died. And if a dream died, it died a long time ago."

"What are you talking about? Is this about your father?"

Yes and no. Maybe it was a little bit about living the life he would have wanted for her. "No, it's about Chuck. I don't think I ever loved him and even he knew that."

Mom clutched her chest. "Really? But you were going to marry him."

"Don't remind me. It's embarrassing." She picked up her cup, the warmth seeping through her fingertips. "He came by the shop and he wants his ring back."

"The nerve!"

At least they were on the same page about that. Because Joanne had a feeling Mom would not agree with the rest of what she had to tell her. If she'd inherited anything from her mother besides her blond hair and fair complexion, it was that longing for everything to remain the same. Mom didn't even want to replace old furniture or rearrange the way it was placed. "If it isn't broken, don't fix it." A common saying from her mother.

Her mother, who had been there for her when Hud broke up with Joanne. When she'd gone out with Matt in retaliation and gotten pregnant with their son. But that was all such a long time ago.

"I have something important to tell you."

"I hope it's not that you've given him the ring back! Not until he pays you back for every last red cent!"

Oh yay! Another thing they agreed on. "That's exactly what I told him."

She shook a finger at Joanne. "Smart."

"But that's not my news. I wanted to tell you, before you heard through the town rumor mill. Hud and I…we're…we're a thing now."

"Hmmm."

So, she'd already heard. "Alright. Who told you?"

"Iris, because remember, she's very good friends with Trish's grandmother. They see each other every week for their knitting circle."

"Oh yeah, that's right." Joanne waited a beat. "Go on. I know you have something to say about me and Hud. Get it off your chest."

"You know how I feel about Hud. I adore him. He's a good friend to you."

"But…?"

"A husband? I don't know. What kind of thirty-two-year old man hasn't ever been married, or even engaged?"

"That's pretty judgy of you. *I've* never been married and I'm thirty-two."

"That's because you wouldn't marry Matt when he gallantly asked you to."

Not this again. "Matt and I never loved each other."

"You should have tried, at least. He was willing to."

But being married as teenagers wouldn't have been the smartest thing to do, either. They'd both been still living with their parents.

"We were teenagers so we would have probably divorced anyway. He was gone all the time."

"I realize that. What you should have done is snatch him up when he came back to town. If you would have, you'd be married to the father of your child now instead of Sarah. Life would be simpler. Safer."

Joanne might have considered it, too, but she and Matt had been angry with each other for so many years. He'd joined the Air Force to help support their son and was gone all the time. She'd appreciated the regular checks but resented doing the tough work herself. For years. Recently, they'd worked hard to coparent and Joanne thought that was about as good as it could get for the two of them. Besides, she really liked Sarah and was happy for them.

"Maybe love can't always be all about security."

"You have a child—of course security comes first. You put Hunter's needs before your own for many years, as you should have. Hud has been available all this time and never found anyone at all?"

"He's dated." She cleared her throat. "Plenty."

"I'm aware." Mom quirked a brow. "And in all those women he couldn't find *one* that was suitable? That tells me that Hud just isn't the settling down type, much as I adore him."

Definitely not what Joanne wanted to hear or believe. "Or maybe he never found the right woman."

"I just don't want you to get hurt again."

"Well, Mom, I'm fresh off a broken engagement with a man who seemed to be perfect for me. He wanted children, he was supposedly saving for our future, he wanted to settle down in Fortune. He played baseball and was afraid to hurt his hands, so he played it safe in every way. And you see how well that worked out."

"Because he was a lying, conniving bastard. You're hurt, and maybe you just need to take some time and consider all your options."

"Funny, that's exactly what I'm doing. And Hud Decker is option number one. I'm tired of playing it safe, and I'm tired of worrying about something that might never happen. I'm still young enough to want sex and passion in my life. And Hud gives me all that. Plus, he takes care of me."

"What do Matt and Hunter have to say about this?"

"Matt is married. Why should I care what he thinks?"

Okay, that sounded a little defensive. But Matt and Sarah were very happy together, and Hunter had eventually become used to the situation. So, maybe he'd get used to Joanne and Hud, too.

"You two have to coparent, after all. And what about Hunter? What does he think?" She paused. "Or does he know?"

"He knows." Joanne finished her coffee, as she fought for time and the right words. "He's not crazy about the idea."

"And he wasn't fond of Chuck, either. Hunter has a good sense about people."

"That's not fair," Joanne protested. "He mentioned that it's always been just the two of us and we don't need anyone else."

Mom nodded. "Maybe for your son, no one is ever going to be good enough."

But Hud was more than good enough for Joanne. She'd made the decision on her own, just by using her mother as a sounding board. The answer was clear, and her heart raced as she clearly understood what she would do going forward. Hopefully everyone was right when they talked about risk equaling reward.

The bigger the risk, the greater the reward.

Chapter Twelve

When Hud arrived for his next rotation a few minutes late, he was in possibly the best mood of his entire life. Because things with Jo were going better than he could have imagined. They'd spent every night that he was off rotation together, either at his place or hers. But even though he was living out many of his fantasies, he wasn't fooling himself. Hunter would be back living with Joanne at the end of the month and their little bubble would burst. They'd both have to deal with a sullen teenager who'd recently had a lot of changes come into his life. Considering that he'd walked in on their first kiss, Hud wanted to make certain *that* didn't happen again.

He kept trying to take them slow, but with their chemistry they were nearly always going from zero to ninety in seconds. He'd be ripping off her clothes or she'd be ripping off his. Jo was enjoying their time together as much as he was, and that was good, but he already wanted much more. And it wasn't going to be easy to get it with both Hunter and Matt still so much a part of Jo's life.

His past preceded him and Hud realized that.

Coldhearted. Detached. Incapable of emotional commitment.

He called bullshit.

Those were just some of the words a few exes had used to describe him. Others, who understood him better, were kinder. Understood. Like Jo. He'd like to believe she understood that he'd been waiting for the right time and the right woman. It finally seemed within his reach and Hud wasn't going to let the damn ring, annoying though it was, ruin this for him. What he'd do was hang in there until Chuck was nothing more than the stink of a memory.

He wasn't going anywhere, and he wouldn't be intimidated. Both Hunter and Matt would have to deal with him.

As he pulled into the station, Hud forced himself to switch gears just as he did when he went home. The pressures and mental stress of the job could be hell on relationships, and he'd seen this firsthand with his friends. Hud was better than most at compartmentalizing, but that didn't mean that it was always easy to leave the stress behind. A forest fire was currently raging out of control in Yuba County and only about 10 percent contained. Wildfire season seemed to be coming earlier every year. The thought of his firefighter brothers, especially the smoke jumpers being dropped into that inferno, was enough to raise his blood pressure.

Hud got out of his truck and did a double take. J.P. was mowing the lawn. While wearing all his protective gear. Turnout pants, boots, tank and breathing apparatus. Hud stopped walking to stare at him. J.P. waved and kept pushing the lawn mower. From time to time, some harmless hazing still happened at the stations. But the directions from the top down had strongly encouraged all hazing to stop. Hud hated to be the killjoy, but damn if he'd let a promotion slip by because of someone's stupid idea of fun.

Hud found Ty, the other lieutenant of Firehouse 57, pouring himself a cup of coffee in the kitchen. Hud hooked his finger toward the window of the house facing outside and the raucous noise of the mower.

"What the hell?"

"We told him he had to get used to carrying around his heavy gear in all kinds of situations. Why not mow the lawn with gear?" Ty shrugged. "He fell for it."

"He's got a tank on, wasting air."

"Gotta learn sometime. Part of this job is thinking for yourself. Why would anyone ask him to mow the lawn wearing full gear? C'mon, he should have known we were joking."

"Go tell him to take off the gear," Hud ordered Alex, who sat quietly at the table.

"Aw, damn." But he got up from the kitchen table and walked outside.

From inside, Hud watched as Alex waved to J.P. until he stopped the mower.

"So. Joanne." Ty continued to sip at his coffee, apparently in no hurry to leave.

"Did you clock out?" Hud pressed.

"Yeah, dude," Ty said. "Never knew you to be such a stickler."

"Things change."

"Yeah? This about Joanne?" Ty asked with a grin.

"What do you mean?"

"Things. Changing. As in you haven't dated in a while. I believe Kristine was the last one, like six months ago? Now Joanne's available. And, if I remember right, I was the one who suggested it could be your moment." Ty thumped his chest with his thumb.

"Proud of yourself?"

"You're the man." Ty fist-bumped with Hud.

"Yeah, yeah." Hud fought a grin. Even these losers could ruin his mood completely.

"Gotta confess, never thought I'd see *you* with a single mom."

"Yeah, but this is Jo. And Hunter. I've known him all his life. He's a great kid."

"But you've never dated his *mother*." Ty set his mug down. "Take it from someone who *has* dated single mothers. Your life is about to change. Radically."

"For me, that's not going to be a bad thing." Hud helped himself to the coffee.

"Yeah?" Ty crossed his arms. "Say goodbye to morning sex. Say goodbye to sex on the kitchen table. Say goodbye to sex in the shower."

Okay, he honestly didn't like the sound of that, but he was a grown-up now. He could wait for privacy, or they could stay over at his place. Except he knew the last thing Jo would want to do is leave a teenager unsupervised for the night with a house all to himself. Even he knew better than to make that rookie mistake.

Hud cleared his throat. "Hunter spends every other weekend with his dad, and some holidays."

"Ah, yes. The baby daddy." Ty held up air quotes. "That's always so much fun, too. You'll be involved, but not really involved."

"Why are you trying to ruin my stellar mood?" He was in a great one, until he saw J.P.

Ty tossed up his hands. "Just trying to be real, bro."

"Just take your 'real' and shove it up your—"

"Yeah, I know where to shove it." Ty put down

his cup and clapped Hud's back. "I'm heading out. Hang in there. Remember she's worth it."

After a few more minutes in which Ty exchanged details on the previous twenty-four shift, blessedly quiet, Ty was off. Hud clocked in and got back to the kitchen with the rest of his crew. J.P. sat at the table in his turnout pants, but without the rest of his heavy gear. He looked no worse for the wear.

"So, whose turn to cook breakfast?" Hud looked at his crew.

They looked back at him, eagerness and expectation in their eyes.

"Yours," they all said at once.

Oh shit.

After a mostly uneventful rotation, Hud worked some overtime, clocked out, showered and headed over to Joanne's because he was taking her to a movie, then she was cooking for him. He figured it wouldn't be anything very exciting. Probably something like roasted chicken and salad. No problem, because he'd brought a dessert, and he would force-feed her if he had to. It was Alex's chocolate mousse cake and it was apparently better than sex—with some people. Alex had sent Hud with a few slices for Hud's "woman." They were all calling Jo that now, and Hud didn't mind. Except for the fact that they probably believed this was business as usual for him. The thrill of the chase. Then the downside that happened when he'd had enough time with a woman and discovered they didn't really connect on anything but a physical level.

At those times, despite what everyone seemed to believe, Hud feared *he* was the unlovable one. This was mixed with the terrible knowledge that he might not ever find anyone who could put up with him. But then he'd assured himself that if he'd really loved Jo, and he had, the possibility of feeling the same for someone else existed. He was capable of loving someone deeply.

It hadn't been until she'd become engaged to Chuck that Hud had an epiphany he'd fought with everything inside him to deny. He'd continued to live in a quagmire of denial as she made wedding preparations. Had agreed that, of course, he'd be *happy* to give her away in the place of her late father. But not until he'd seen Jo in the wedding dress had Hud realized the wedding would actually *happen*. He was too damn late and had missed his window. She'd marry Chuck, and Hud would have to support that.

So, in a way, he should really thank Chuck for backing out. Hell, maybe he would someday. Thanks to him, Hud had a second chance.

Hud pulled his truck up to the curb in front of Joanne's home. The lights were on inside and as he shut off his headlights, he saw her in the kitchen window, head bent over the sink. The light reflected in her pale blond hair, and she tucked a stray behind her ear, biting her lip in the way she did when she was entirely focused.

The scene felt domestic, something he'd always resisted because it felt like a general loss of freedom. But the facts were that he'd been long ago domesticized by Jo without quite realizing it. The only thing that had been missing in their best friend's style of domesticity was the romance. The sex. With that thought, he shut off the truck and hightailed it to her front door. The sooner they got done with the movie, the sooner they'd be back in bed.

At the door, he handed her the cake. "From Alex. Claims it's better than sex."

She made a face, her nose wrinkled. "I'll put this in the fridge and just grab my purse."

They were going to see some kind of romance book made into a movie, and of course, he was fine with that in this new, supportive boyfriend role. At one time he would have voted this one down and they'd have settled on something between a rom-com and science fiction. Usually that meant some kind of foreign film with subtitles.

"This is supposed to be a three-hanky movie," she said, strapping on her seat belt.

"What's that supposed to mean?" He pulled out on to the street leading to The Granada, the only movie theater in town.

"Really, Hud? Three hankies? As in you'll go through three handkerchiefs with all your tears."

He cringed. "I don't want to sit in a movie theater with you crying about fictional characters."

"Why not? That's when you get to hold me and make it all better."

When she put it that way…

But halfway through the movie, Hud was irritated because the hero was a firefighter. Apparently, no one hired consultants anymore because said hero was in a structure fire with the same kind of eyesight and vision as he would have on a gorgeous day at the beach. Yeah. Not going to happen. Smoke was usually so thick you literally couldn't see your hand in front of you. But when the firefighter ripped off his mask, once outside, to give the heroine "oxygen" he wanted to stand up and walk out. He would have, had it not been for Jo's arm linking through his, holding his hand while with the other she held a tissue.

He leaned close to whisper. "Our tanks have air in them, not oxygen. The same air that's all around them now that she's *outside*."

"Shhh."

"It makes no sense." He shook his head.

At last the movie ended and they made their way out of the crowded theater. Outside, he stopped and wiped away a smudge from under her eyes, caused by her tears. Then he tugged Jo into a sideways hug, and they walked together hip to hip. His mind was on a light dinner and then bed.

"Hud!"

He turned at the sound of the female voice calling out his name and cringed. Joanne stopped beside him.

It was Kristine, with a group of her friends.

"Hey, you two." She eyed them, lingering on the tight embrace, a hint of mischief in her eyes. "So good to *see* you."

"Hi, Kristine," Joanne said. "How are you doing?"

"Not as good as you." Kristine grinned at Hud and crossed her arms. "I *really* hate to say I told you so, but…when was I going to get that call?"

"Yeah." Hud knew exactly what she meant. "Soon."

He felt every one of Jo's low back muscles when they tensed under his touch. But even if what Kristine had said sounded suspicious, he didn't want to stand in a public parking lot with her and Jo and have to explain himself. Especially not when the subject would be referring to when he'd grown the balls to admit he'd always been in love with Jo.

"I guess I shouldn't be surprised to run into one of your exes every time we go out," Jo said once they were in the truck. "But I always liked Kristine."

"She liked you, too."

"What did she mean? Why do you have to call her?"

"Jo, I said I'd be exclusive, and I meant it."

"I know, and I trust you. Does this mean you're not going to tell me?"

"Okay, okay." He fought a grin. "Kristine always thought you had a thing for me but couldn't admit it. Told me to call her and let her know when you finally wised up that you're crazy about me."

"Why do I think that's not exactly the way that went down?" She laughed. "I told you, I *like* Kristine."

In front of her house, he shut off the engine and released his tight grip on the steering wheel. Took a breath. "Okay, so maybe it was the reverse."

"Hud." She spoke softly. Sweetly. She unbuckled her seat belt and reached across the console for him. "I'm crazy about you, too."

This was nuts. It was too soon, and yet it wasn't soon enough. Madness, mayhem, and also the most logical thing in his world. He pressed his forehead to hers.

"Look. I can go as slow as you want with us. But I'm also ready to leapfrog over everything in our way. For years, we've had people come between us. First Matt, then Hunter. Your mother."

"My mother?"

"It's no secret that she always wanted you with Matt, after you had Hunter. Thank God for Sarah, so now Matt's no longer even an option."

She threaded her fingers through his hair. "He never was. I love Matt as the father of my child and that's all. I was never in love with him."

"Now we've got *Chuck*. But I'll wait as long as it

takes for you to get over him. For you to be ready to give him back that ring and move forward with me."

Jo pulled back to meet his gaze, her fingers loosening their hold in his hair. "Baby, no. You don't need to even think about *him* anymore. I'm giving back the ring. I decided."

"Yeah? But how will you get the money from him?"

"Maybe I'll sue. I don't know yet, but I'll find another way."

It was on the tip of his tongue to offer to pay for it all, but he knew Jo would hate that. He had the money and could afford to. But so did Jo and that was hardly the point.

"Or, you know, maybe I'll just let it go. It's only money, right? Maybe it's better to have him out of our life for good, like you said."

He didn't miss the "our life" instead of "my life" and it kick-started his heart.

"I hate to say this, but you know that I could pay him a visit. He's afraid of me."

"For good reason. But you shouldn't have to do that." She rubbed her cheek against his jaw. "I will keep it as an option, though."

Because Hud wondered how Chuck could ever be out of her life without paying her back. The irritation would always be in the back of her mind, but with some luck, in time it would fade. Hud could fill her mind and life with many other distractions. Trips. More picnics. Lots and lots of great sex.

Until one day the guy would be nothing more than an unpleasant memory.

Chapter Thirteen

Oh, my heart.

Hud had believed that she wasn't going to get over Chuck anytime soon, and he was willing to wait until she did. Until she was ready to give back the stupid ring even without getting any money back. Knowing how Hud felt about the ring in the first place, she didn't think she'd ever loved him as much as she did in that moment.

She sealed her words and thoughts with a kiss, which he then took over, and they both quickly got wild and out of control, fogging up the windows. Her hand was on his muscular thigh while he got handsy under her bra, tweaking a nipple and making her moan. The console between them was hardly a match for their determination. She pressed against him, her elbow bumping a visor and then the rearview mirror. They still acted like a couple of horny teenagers.

God, she hoped that would never change.

Then, either Hud or she accidentally pressed the horn, and she jumped.

He burst into laughter. "I think we can afford to go inside now. We don't have to do this in a car anymore."

She agreed, but there was also something so memorable about these moments alone. The memories were warm and thrilling. They slid into her heart and plundered deep. He'd always meant excitement to her. Danger. As a teenager she'd been so attracted to that. Now here was this grown man that to her meant safety as much as frenzy. Passion. The combination never failed to enthrall her. Swept away in his kisses, she forgot anything painful had ever happened. He never failed to stoke her desires to fiery levels.

Always, there was a kind of ease between them. Like they'd been together, this way, for years instead of days.

Inside, he led her to the bedroom, where he pulled off his shirt. No one wore a shirt like Hudson Decker did, but shirtless Hud was a sight to behold. She wasn't ever going to get tired of running the pads of her fingers over those hard planes and granite muscles.

She did so now and loved the way they bunched under her touch. "I wish we could always feel this way."

He met her gaze, eyes hot and serious. "Maybe it's possible, with the right person."

She turned, giving him her back and he slowly slid down the zipper of her dress. He nuzzled her neck as it slowly slid to the floor in a puddle at her feet.

"If not with you, then I don't think it's possible for me." She stepped out of her dress and into his arms.

His rough large hands slid up and down her spine, leaving trails of tingles. "It's possible."

They seemed to move slower tonight, his fierceness held just below the surface, or tamed. One finger looped under the strap of her bra and he slipped it down, cupping her breast. He bent low to cover it with his mouth, sucking almost reverently through the silky material. When he uncovered it and took in her nipple, the sensation of his mouth and hot tongue directly on her naked skin made her gasp.

He moved lower and then lower still, falling to his knees as he kissed her belly button and lingered there. His hands cupped her behind, squeezing as his tongue teased around the line of her sheer panties. She could barely hold a moan in as he lowered them, spreading her thighs. He licked and stroked her folds until she was a quivering mess, holding on to his shoulders, barely able to keep herself upright on limp and useless legs.

Holding on to her butt, he lifted her and set her on the bed where she went to her knees and pulled him close by the loop of his pants.

"These need to come off," she said, kissing his pec as she worked his buckle.

"Way ahead of you, baby."

His hands were a lot faster than hers and he stepped out of his pants and boxer briefs, the evidence clear that he was just as ready as she was. He took a condom from the nightstand, quickly ripped it and slipped it on. Then he rolled on top of her, his warm and strong body covering hers.

"Hmm. I won't ever get tired of this. You, naked. Stay that way for me, would you?"

"I'll try." She wrapped her legs around him, feeling his hardness as he pressed against her belly.

In the next moment, he braced above her and thrust inside her. As he went deeper, she reached for him, touching him everywhere her hands could reach, urging him faster. The bed creaked under the force of their weight and lovemaking.

"Jo, baby. So good."

"Yes, yes. Oh, Hud." He swallowed her moan with a deep kiss. In the next moment she crested that powerful and intense wave of pleasure rippling through her, as she trembled and shook with her release.

A few more strokes and Hud groaned his own pleasure.

They were both out of breath and sweaty as they

collapsed in each other's arms, spent. Joanne burrowed her face in his warm neck and threw her leg over his, trying to catch her breath. Trying to make sense out of her feelings.

Because the warmth that seeped into her heart was caused by more than an orgasm. More to do with his taking care of her first, always certain she'd enjoy herself as much as he did. It had to do with something deeper. Rarer. She loved him. Admired the man that he'd become. A man who put his friends first, who even put the welfare of others above his own in his chosen profession.

But far from the reckless kid he'd been, she could now see he only took calculated risks. He'd never walk into a fire unprepared or without an exit plan. He didn't make rash decisions out of anger. His temper was righteous and controlled. And above all she trusted him more than she ever had any other man in her life except her father. The *L* word had scared Hud once before and it might again. She didn't think so, not this time, but she had to know. The sooner the better.

Especially when her body buzzed and pulsed with the desire to tell him how much he meant to her.

She disentangled from his arms and sat, keeping the covers over her breasts. "I want to tell you something, but you have to *promise* me you won't freak out."

"Promise." His brow furrowed in concern. "But

the way you pulled away from me right now is freak-ing me out."

At one time, he might not have been mature enough to tell her that. She appreciated the way he'd grown into his emotions. He was comfortable in his skin. She let out a deep breath. This time she could say the words and know they didn't have any con-ditions or expectations attached to them. He didn't have to love her or change her life. He owed her nothing in return.

She was strong without him, but even stronger with him.

"It's because what I have to tell you is serious. And I didn't want you think I'd say this because you have such a great body. Because you do, of course. Or that I'd tell you this because you're such a great lover. Which, of course, you are. But you know that." Now she was rambling.

"Spit it out, Jo." He narrowed his eyes.

She met his eyes. "I love you."

He reached for her, a smile on his lips, his mouth already forming a word, but she stopped him with a finger on his lips. "Shh. Wait. You don't have to say anything, okay? Just sit with it. Know it."

He quirked a brow until she lowered her finger from his mouth. "Whatever you say. But this is me, *not* freaking out."

She had to laugh. "Look at us, all grown-up."

"The second time around is better, or so I hear."

"That's true, I think." She climbed out of bed and sprinted toward the bathroom. "Meet me in the shower and let me see if the second time around tonight is even better."

"Right behind you."

And in fact, he almost got to the shower before she did.

The next morning, Jo rolled and stretched like a cat. Hud was not next to her in bed, but she heard sounds in the kitchen. Smelled the aroma of freshly brewed coffee and practically salivated. Heard the sizzle of butter in a pan. He was banging around in her kitchen, making them breakfast. A man who'd already captured her heart, simply showing off now.

Yes, I love you. When are you going to stop being so perfect?

"Hud? Coffee, please," she moaned in her caffeine-deprived state, wondering if she should bother to get dressed.

Lately, she enjoyed her constant state of nakedness around the house.

"Stay there," he called out. "I'll bring it."

There was not much point in dressing when everything would come off sooner rather than later. When Hud was around—and lately that was every day that he wasn't with his crew—she pretty much lived in her fuzzy bathrobe and nothing else. Soon enough this kind of lifestyle would change. Hunter would be home in another week and life would return to normal. She'd take off her lover hat and put on her boring mother-of-a-teenager hat. She had no doubt that Hud would stick around, but no idea what their new situation would look like. He'd have to be patient and understand that she was a mother and couldn't always drop everything for him.

And Hud probably wasn't used to that in any other of his prior relationships. Why would he be? He hadn't even dated another single mother. "Too complicated," he'd once said, another red flag and reason she thought they would never work. Either he'd apparently changed his mind about "complicated" or he just had no *idea* what he would be walking into. It was one thing to be her son's friend and pseudo uncle, but this new and complicated relationship was going to be tough on everyone.

Joanne rolled on her back, and a moment later heard the front door slam. Then her son's voice. "You're always here!"

Oh. My. God. Code three! Or whatever first responders said when it was an emergency. Joanne leaped out of bed and shut her bedroom door, locked it, then proceeded to put on as many clothes as she could find. Quickly. She could hear only muffled voices now, Hud's deeper more commanding voice, followed by her son's. It was imperative that she get out there, stat, and explain. Fix this. Maybe she could say that Hud slept on the couch and was making them breakfast. She'd slept in. In her clothes, of course. She'd slept in her clothes. That was her story and she was sticking to it.

"Hi, honey," Joanne said, walking into the kitchen. "I heard you come in."

But Hud stood in the middle of the kitchen, shirtless, wearing nothing but his jeans, low on his hips. He gave her a little smirk and shrugged.

Walking past her, he stopped to press a kiss against her temple. "Going to put on a shirt."

"Good idea," she said on a sigh.

Hunter glared at her, looking disgusted. "I came by to have you sign a permission slip." He threw it on the counter.

"Fine," she said, taking out a pen to sign it, and barely looking at it. Some kind of field trip. Matt's signature was already on it. She handed it back. "I'm sorry we shocked you."

He snorted. "I'm not shocked."

"I would have told you about us, but I was waiting until you came back home from your dad's."

"This is how it's going to be now? Hud always over here? Is he moving in?"

She held up a palm. "Okay, slow down. We haven't talked about a lot of these things. No, he's not moving in."

"Because Chuck never even lived here. Our house is too small."

It wasn't much smaller than Matt and Sarah's,

ironically, and that seemed to be just fine with Hunter. Joanne would be upset by the double standard, but she'd set it up this way. She'd never really had a man in the house, wanting Hunter to feel comfortable in their home. Never threatened. Chuck was to have been the first man to live with them. Her husband. Now she wondered why she'd made it so easy for Hunter to accept the fact that she'd always been alone. Yet Matt was already married and even before he had been, Sarah had lived with him.

"I don't want you to get upset, but this is how it's going to be. Hud and I...we're in a relationship. You'll have to get used to that."

"I'm not going to get *used* to it. First Chuck, now Hud. What if Hud leaves you at the altar too?"

"Whoa. You are getting way ahead of yourself."

"Well, I don't want to live here anymore if Hud's *always* going to be around."

"That's not fair. Your dad has Sarah and you don't seem to mind that."

"Yeah, we all get along okay. Maybe I should go live there."

Fear pierced through Joanne at the thought that her only child would leave her home. *Her* home, where she could keep him safe from harm and life altering mistakes.

"No, you shouldn't." Joanne fought to keep her cool. "You belong here. That hasn't changed."

"Yeah? If you want to be with Hud, then maybe I

want to go live with my dad." He turned to go, and it was then that she heard keys jiggling in his pockets.

"Wait. Don't you need a ride back? I'll let you drive."

"No need," he said, holding up car keys. "I got my license two days ago. Dad let me borrow the car."

"You got your license? *Already?*"

Why would Matt do this? It had been six months since Hunter had obtained his permit, but they were supposed to talk over these kinds of huge decisions together. Coparent. As usual, he was the popular parent. She was the uncool, conservative, nutrition-minded, strict parent.

"Why not? I already had the driving hours logged in, and the test was super easy. Sarah took me. Passed on the first try."

Oh, of course he had! Her son was a genius when he wanted to be. Joanne crossed her arms. "I'm going to talk to your father about this. He should have run it by me."

"Great!" Hunter rolled his eyes and then he was out the door, hand held up in a half wave.

Joanne ran to the window to watch him drive off, half expecting him to peal out in anger. But her son didn't do anything of the sort. He drove Matt's SUV slowly down the cul-de-sac. And then Hud's strong arms were around her, pulling her back to him, dipping his head in the crook of her shoulder.

"I'll talk to him."

"I'm sorry. You didn't sign up for this drama."

"Yeah, I did. I signed up for it all." He turned her to face him. "I'm going to make this better. Whatever it takes, I'm going to make us work. He may not like it at first, but he'll get used to me being around here more often."

"Maybe we shouldn't shove it in his face that we're sleeping together."

"Probably a good idea, but too late on that one."

She plunked her forehead to his chest, groaning. "I know."

"Leave it to me, baby. He's not leaving your home. I'll fix this."

Chapter Fourteen

The next day, Joanne made arrangements to meet Chuck in a public place and give him back the ring. She chose the coffee and pastry shop in town, The Drip, and he agreed easily, probably not wanting a scene.

He was already seated when she arrived and gave her a forced smile. "Joanne."

"Hey there. Joanne is glad that Chuck is here on time." Sue her, she couldn't resist.

Chuck simply blinked. Maybe he now realized how stupid he sounded. "Again, I'm sorry."

Oh yes, yes, she'd forgotten. That fixed everything. He was *sorry*.

"You don't have to keep saying that." She fished in her purse for the ring and planted it in front of him. "There."

He picked the ring up and palmed it. "Thanks. What made you change your mind?"

"Hud convinced me."

"I figured he would have something to do with it." Chuck frowned. "He's always there, isn't he?"

Joanne briefly considered telling Chuck that he resembled a sullen teenage boy at the moment, then decided she wouldn't go there. When he and Hunter had been together, she'd dealt with two difficult "boys" making her feel like a mediator half the time. Chuck had claimed to like Hunter and want more children, but he'd hardly even *tried* to get along with Hunter.

I've been such an idiot. Why was I even marrying Chuck?

It hurt to believe she'd been so desperate not to wind up alone. But with a son who had one foot out the door, it was true that she'd made stupid snap decisions. It was time to stop making those. And if this didn't work out again with Hud and she wound up alone for the rest of her life, she'd somehow deal. Because no matter what happened, she wasn't settling for less than everything. Never again.

"Look, I don't care what you think of Hud. The point is, *you* did a lousy thing. Do you have any idea how humiliating this all has been for me?"

"Not really." He shrugged.

"My business has suffered because of you. Brides tend to be a superstitious group. Just like baseball players. The real reason I'm giving you back the ring is that I don't want Hud to believe I haven't moved on, because I have."

Joanne had been in the bridal industry for over a decade, and she'd heard it all through the grapevine. Everything from bridesmaids getting caught making out with the groom before the wedding, to a last-minute hurrah between the bride and her ex. Caught on video. The actual wedding day could get crazy when one mixed drinking with latent desires of the heart.

Not to mention the marriage itself, when the bride forced herself to ignore the man she really wanted, for the only one she thought she could have.

Sometimes taking a risk was the best choice.

"How are you, otherwise?" Chuck asked. "I think about you sometimes."

"Please don't."

"Hate to say I told you so." He scowled. "I heard you're with Hud now."

"Yes, we're together. You were right. Happy now?"

"Not really."

"How's Mandy doing? I keep hearing her song on the radio. 'I'm Sick of You' or something. I'm sure it's not autobiographical."

"Yeah, we broke up."

They'd broken up. Good thing she'd given him back that lousy ring when she couldn't very well bribe him with it to get her money back.

"Well, I guess… I'm sorry?"

"I think she wanted to marry a ballplayer because J.Lo. married a ballplayer. I guess ballplayers were in season but now she's on to a football player."

"I don't know, Chuck, that sounds pretty shallow of her."

"Right?" He reached for her hand. "You were the best thing that ever happened to me."

"No." She removed her hand. "I wasn't. I could have been your worst nightmare. I didn't love you or make room for you in my life. We didn't even live together because I didn't want you crowding Hunter. Crowding me. I have no idea what I was thinking. Maybe I thought you'd slide into my life, I'd give you a drawer, and we'd keep your stuff in the shed or something."

"You wanted to get married. That's *all* you wanted."

"That's the first thing you've said in a long time that I agree with."

Chuck reached in the back of his pants pocket and set a check on the table. It was made out to her, a sum big enough to cover more than his half of the wedding.

She grabbed it. "How did you manage?"

"I sold the BMW that Mandy bought me."

Joanne gaped. "She bought you a BMW?"

"Yeah," he said, looking morose. "When I was her man. But if I hadn't sold it, she would probably be taking it back."

"Good thinking, I guess."

"You deserve it. If I'm being honest here, I think you still would have been a good deal for me. I would have taken the drawer. I would have kept my stuff in the shed."

"Chuck, that's ridiculous. We both deserved better."

"You've got yours now. Maybe someday I'll get mine."

It was probably that kicked puppy-dog look in his brown eyes, but Joanne squeezed his hand. "I was so mad at you, and I still think it was a lousy thing to do. But now I have to thank you for saving me from making the worst mistake of my life."

Later at the boutique, Joanne forced her thoughts away from Hunter's driver's license debacle back to the designs she'd been working on for Leah. It had at least served to distract her from the Taylors.

"Why is the dress blue?" Nora leaned to look over Joanne's shoulder.

"My bride wants blue."

Nora wrinkled her nose. "For real? A second marriage or something?"

"Or something. It's actually a romantic story." Joanne reiterated everything she'd learned from Leah and her fiancé, also known as her ex-husband.

"How sweet," Nora said, carrying a dress to the front. "Jill is coming in today for her dress, so prepare for a lot of gushing and possibly some tears."

"Aw, she's so sweet and in love."

"Right? It should have been a clue to me when you were so matter-of-fact about your dress," Nora said.

Ignoring that, she handed over the sketch pad to Nora. "What do you think?"

"I love the sweetheart collar."

"This blue is going to be a challenge. I have to find just the right type of material to make it work."

"Oh hey, don't want to freak you out or anything, but I got stuck at the light on Barrett this morning and I could have sworn I saw Hunter driving to school. By himself. Just thought you should know. It takes a village and all that."

"He got his license."

Nora froze. "And you're not having a major freakout?"

"I'm not happy about it. They went behind my back. I mean, I got voted down that he should get his license at sixteen, but I had no idea he'd do it the month he's staying with his father."

"Yeah, that wasn't cool." Nora hung Jill's dress and began unwrapping it. "But look at you, all calm and collected. I know how difficult this is for you."

"Maybe because I have bigger worries."

"Bigger than being jilted, or having your sixteen-year-old let loose on the unsuspecting public roads?"

"I can't even believe I'm saying this but yes. Last night, Hunter showed up to the house unexpectedly and…well, let's just say he now knows Hud and I are sleeping together."

"He caught you in the act?" Nora covered her mouth.

"Okay, thank you for reminding me that it could always be worse. No, but Hud was in the kitchen making me breakfast. Without a shirt on."

"Well, at least he had his pants on." She paused. "Please say he had his pants on."

"He did."

"How did Hud react when you made him leave? Is he pissed off?"

"I didn't make him leave."

"You didn't?" Nora said. "Remember that time Chuck was over and when Hunter showed up you had Chuck leave out the back door?"

"Oh yeah. Well, it hadn't been six months." Joanne cleared her throat. "Hunter didn't stay long anyway. He said he might move in with Matt if Hud and I are going to be together."

"Manipulative little man, isn't he?"

Joanne scoffed. "It's not going to happen. I'm talking to Matt today."

"Pretty sure he doesn't want Hunter living with

him and Sarah and disrupting his privacy. He is a newlywed, after all."

"Yeah, I'm pretty sure Matt now appreciates what I've been through for years. Having a teenager is not all that different from having a toddler when it comes to privacy. But I'm used to it."

"Hud isn't."

"I know."

That worried Joanne. Maybe after a few months of the teenage drama he'd get tired of being put in second place. But she'd have to work on that. Achieve a balance. She deserved a love life and that's why bedroom locks had been invented.

"But he said he'll talk to Hunter."

"Those two used to get along fine. I'm sure that's all it takes. A nice, long talk man to little man."

Joanne snorted. "Hunter hates when you call him 'little man.' He is six feet tall now."

"I've known the rug rat since he was two. He's little man to me, always."

Once Jill came in the store for one last fitting, Nora and Joanne dropped everything else. The boutique was infused with the special magic of a bride one step closer to her wedding date. One of Joanne's favorite moments and Jill did not disappoint. She arrived with her mother, and her good friends Carly and Zoey, who was now her sister-in-law, too.

Nora poured flutes of champagne while Joanne handed out tissues from the box she kept handy.

"You look amazing!" Zoey said, wiping her cheeks.

"Like a fairy tale princess," her mother said, grabbing a tissue and dabbing her eyes. "Doesn't she look like a princess, girls?"

"She does," everyone answered, practically in harmony.

It was time for Joanne to set the stage. This time she got Sam's name right, thank you God, as she described the way that Jill would walk toward her groom during their outdoor wedding. Everyone seemed enthralled by Joanne's description, but a funny thing happened. She didn't get anyone's name wrong, but the bride she pictured wasn't Jill. It was Joanne. And she found herself describing her own perfect wedding day.

The one she'd longed for when she was a young girl but hadn't allowed herself to dream about for years. And this time, the man she walked toward was the one she'd wanted for what felt like half of her life. Hud, looking incredibly handsome in his tux, his green eyes shimmering and matching the cummerbund perfectly. Just as she'd imagined they would.

After everyone had left, and Nora ran off to make dinner for her boyfriend, Joanne was left alone with her thoughts. She should close up the shop and head home, where she expected Hud for dinner. Because she wanted to see him, of course, but first she needed to get a grip. She couldn't do this to him. It wasn't fair to be thinking about marriage again so soon. She'd just fallen in love with him.

They were just getting to know each other again and already finding obstacles. Hunter wasn't ready. Her mother thought Joanne should still be somewhere in the seven-step grieving process. And God only knew what Matt would say about all this. She might just be the only one ready in this scenario. Ready for her life to begin. The one she'd kept on hold for years while she lied to herself about Hud. While she pretended being his friend was enough for her.

So much wasted time!

"Joanne?"

The door to her shop jingled announcing someone had stepped inside, and there stood Matt Conner.

Straight out of her fantasy into cold, harsh reality. Why not? She lived on the corner of Reality and Sensibility and her address still hadn't changed.

"Hey there. I was going to call you, but the day got away from me."

Not for the first time, it made Joanne's heart ache to see how much Hunter resembled his father. Matt was almost as good-looking as Hud. Her son had really lucked out in the gene pool. He had the same tall frame, long legs, dark hair and square jaw. He'd apparently inherited his father's high IQ, as well. But mostly, she was simply grateful that Matt was a good man and someday their son would be, too.

So many times, she wished she could have loved him. Tried. Despite the fact that she and Matt hadn't always been friends, he'd been right about so many things that she was only now starting to realize. She'd kept such control over Hunter's life and put him at the center of her life for so long that when it came time to put herself first, she'd almost forgotten how to make wise, well-thought-out choices. To balance her own needs with those of her family.

Matt stuck his hands in his pockets. "I should have told you about the appointment at the DMV. Don't blame Sarah. I was called to a last-minute chartered flight and Hunter begged us not to reschedule."

"Maybe I overreacted. I knew he'd be getting his license soon."

"We should have given you a heads-up."

"It would have been nice. But honestly, that's not what bothers me the most about our son right now."

"He's a good kid. You did a great job with him."

"But I'm afraid I let Hunter mistakenly believe he could call the shots in my life. I gave him too much control at some point. Then when I took my life back, I made a huge mistake."

"I'm sure that's not true."

"Really? *Chuck* was a huge mistake."

He shrugged. "Well…"

"Yeah." She couldn't help a strained laugh. "*He* was a mistake. But Hud isn't. Now our son has just informed me that if I keep seeing him, he'll move in with you and Sarah."

Matt quirked a brow. "That's not going to happen."

"Miss your privacy already?" she teased.

"It isn't easy, but I also know that's not what you want. So, it's true. You're seeing Hud."

God, she hoped Matt wouldn't be giving her a hard time about this, too. She was tired of people putting themselves between her and Hud. Now that she'd moved herself out of her own way, if she had to bulldoze through every single other person who had doubts, she would. It was her time to be happy. Finally.

She crossed her arms. "Is that a problem?"

"Why would it be? Look. You and I both know that Hunter derailed our lives."

"Don't say that. *We* derailed our lives. By being young and stupid. Irresponsible."

"You're right. But here's the thing. Maybe it's time Hunter heard about our complicated history. Our very weird triangle."

Joanne had decided that she'd never tell Hunter, because that was grown-up stuff that didn't concern him. He already knew enough. Understood that his parents had been young and foolish. That they hadn't planned on him but still wanted and loved him very much. But telling him about Hud…and that Matt was a complete rebound. She didn't want her son to think less of her. Or less of his father.

"I don't know."

"He might understand why Hud has never liked me. If you think he doesn't sense that tension between us, you're kidding yourself."

"What do you mean? Hud likes you fine."

Matt rolled his eyes. "Hunter's growing up fast, and I think it's time we told him the truth."

"I've never wanted to involve him in any of my drama." Yet that had happened anyway thanks to Chuck.

"You don't have to give him all of the details, but if he knew that you and Hud had a prior relationship...that you might have wound up together—"

"Except for him? No, I can't do that to my son."

"I was going to say that he might understand why Hud is so important to you."

"I'll think about it. But I'm glad we can all agree that Hunter *isn't* going to move in with you and Sarah."

Matt nodded. "I agree. That was fairly manipulative of him, and he and I will have a long talk about it."

"Thanks." Joanne blew out a breath. "I'm actually glad you retired from the Air Force. It was hard giving up all the control, but it's something I needed to do. And I understand that now."

"Sometimes you worry too much, but no one can

blame you. I certainly can't." Matt's gaze swept over her with kindness.

She knew he was thinking about her father's untimely death. Her teenage pregnancy. Hud's car accident. His enlistment in the Army. It had all shaped her life in many ways.

"I appreciate that. More than you know."

"You do realize that Hunter is worried about you? Like mother, like son. I mean, you were supposed to be married less than a month ago. He's heard the small-town rumors about the bad luck boutique."

She hadn't thought of it that way. "Did he ask you?"

"He did and I told him the truth. He was worried about you. That's why he's so resistant to Hud," Matt continued. "He's thinking you're going to get hurt all over again."

"But Hud has always been there for us."

"Well, maybe that's part of the problem. It's the newly defined relationships that are bothering him. Because he doesn't understand how it all happened so quickly. But he would, if he had a few more details to see the full picture. If he knew how long this has been going on."

Matt had a point.

"I'll talk to him, too," Joanne said. "Because Hud and I are in a relationship and it's serious. And *no one* is going to change my mind about him."

Matt smiled. "It's about damn time."

Chapter Fifteen

The next night, Joanne couldn't sleep and woke in the middle of the night. A million thoughts swam to the forefront of her mind, disrupting her peace, demanding attention. Hunter. The driver's license. Getting the wedding money from Chuck. The Taylor wedding and that whole debacle. Leah and the perfect dress she wanted but actually couldn't afford. It didn't help that Hud had pulled an extra shift and would be gone all night. She'd already grown so used to sleeping with him that her bed felt huge and empty without him. Her bedroom was covered in his delicious manly scent. Leather and the soap he used. His divine cologne. He had clothes in her drawers and spare uniforms in the closet. Boots under her bed.

For so long, she'd resisted a man taking over her home but now she didn't know how she'd lived all these years without Hud being the one to take up all the empty spaces.

"Come on up, Rachel. It's okay." Joanne patted the foot of her bed, a place Rachel was rarely allowed.

She happily bounced up, wagging her tail and turning in a circle until she found just the right spot. Then she let out a happy dog sigh. Rachel stayed with Joanne all the time now because Hud was over so much. It no longer made sense to spend all that money on doggy day care, so he only sent her when they were both working.

"It's just us girls tonight."

She felt unsettled. Something had been bothering her about the Taylor wedding. The designs she'd created were good, but not her best work. The problem, she now believed, was that she hadn't really known Brenda well enough to design the right dress. She hadn't asked enough questions, or maybe just not the right ones. Her romance with the groom had been nothing inspiring. They'd met at a law firm in Silicon Valley and their first date had been an all-night trial prep session. Not too romantic.

Joanne grabbed her sketch pad from the nightstand and paged through her recent drawings. She found the dress she'd drawn a few days ago thinking it might work for Leah. But Joanne had realized almost immediately the dress was far too avant-garde for her. It had straight, almost severe lines, with a plunging back. A short train and shorter veil. Sophisticated. Daring and unorthodox. Only a chic bride could wear a dress such as this one. Joanne didn't even know how the concept had come out of her, but like so many of her ideas, it had surprised her. She would certainly never make such a bold statement on *her* wedding day.

No. It definitely wouldn't work for sweet Leah, but Brenda Taylor immediately came to mind.

Joanne didn't know which of her designs they'd settled on, but she knew that this one was far superior than the ones they'd purchased. She could keep the design, because sooner or later she'd have a bride it would fit. But the truth was that she wanted Brenda to have it. All the bitterness Joanne felt at being passed over had dissipated. If the Taylors thought she'd bring bad luck to their wedding day, it was simply because they had no idea that she was in a much better place right now. Far from bad luck, the wedding day fail had been one of the best things ever to happen to her.

And maybe it was high time for them to witness that much better, far richer Joanne.

The plan had come to Hud while on a boring shift where the only calls that had come in were medical ones.

Genius idea number one: he would take Hunter rock climbing at Wildfire Ridge Outdoor Adventures. There was no other sport that required more trust between two people than rock climbing. In some cases, the relationship with a partner could mean the difference between life or death. Hud would demonstrate once more that he trusted this rangy sixteen-year-old, who, let's face it, was like a son to him.

Like a son. If this worked out permanently with Jo, and each day and night brought him more hope that it would, he'd have a stepson. A ready-made family. While he'd always been a friend to Hunter, Jo had called the shots with her son. It was how she'd wanted it. She rarely wanted his advice, but he gave it to her anyway: Give him short bursts of freedom so he learns how to handle himself. Respect the fact that he might need some privacy. *Yes, let him get his license when he's sixteen. I actually agree with Matt.* Understand that he's no longer your little boy.

She'd listened, because he'd pulled the best friend card. Hell, there was no one that understood teenage boys better than a former teenage boy. And Hud had been a hell of a teenage boy. He felt sorry for his parents now, who'd done the best they could with him. But he'd been born to parents who hadn't given him *enough* freedom. By the time they did, he went crazy with it. When he'd discovered sex, it had been like being handed the keys to an ice-cream parlor with sixty-five different flavors. How was he supposed to pick just one? How did he even know what he liked? Shouldn't he at least try them all out once?

That kind of idiocy, the inability to appreciate what he had, was how he'd lost Jo.

Determined that Hunter would not be a stupid kid too, he was ready to enlighten him. He was probably worried that Hud would also hurt his mother, and after the recent events, he couldn't blame him.

So, on Saturday after his shift rotation, he picked Hunter up at his father's house.

"Can I drive?" Hunter asked when he came up to the driver's side window. "I need the practice and you've been driving like…forever, right?"

Hud moved to the passenger seat. "Why not?"

Hunter drove to the outskirts of Fortune and the hill leading to Wildfire Ridge. They'd been here together many times. Hunter liked coming along to occasionally bend Sam Hawker's ear, Jill's fiancé, and one of the many guides here. He'd been a former Marine and Hunter was still at the age where that highly impressed him. But he'd also been on several ride-alongs with Hud, and they'd talked Army and all things military. Growing up in a small town that had at some point become a haven for former military, it wasn't surprising that Hunter wanted to serve.

Hud just wanted to know it was for the right reasons, and he knew Matt and Sam agreed with him.

Hud relaxed in the passenger seat, until Hunter

nearly missed stopping at a red light in time. The tires screeched. Hud didn't even blink.

"You know about my accident?"

Hunter snorted. "Only because my mom told me like a hundred zillion times. She said that's when you decided to be a first responder."

"You never heard my side of the story."

"Was it something stupid? Like you ran a red light?" He cleared his throat. "I'm not used to the brakes on your truck."

"No, I lost control of my father's sports car. Going way too fast."

"Your dad had a sports car? Kewl."

"Don't get too excited. It was an old classic Mustang. But a very sweet ride."

"Was the accident your fault or someone else's?"

"I wrapped the car around a tree, so I guess you could say that's my fault."

No one had ever shared the gory details with Hunter and Hud wasn't about to do that now. Sometimes fears could be just as powerful as misguided courage. And just as harmful. Hunter didn't say anything, apparently using all his attention to make a left turn against traffic.

Impressed, Hud didn't continue talking until he'd safely turned. "And it happened over a girl."

Concentration broken, Hunter glanced at him for a second, then back to the road. "Huh."

"She wasn't just *any* girl to me. I loved her. I was

angry because *I'd* done something stupid. So, she went out with another guy. I was jealous. Don't drive when you're jealous."

Hunter snorted. "Or mad."

"Just kidding. Sometimes you have to drive when you're mad or jealous."

"Yeah. Or I might never drive."

"Exactly. Just make sure to separate your emotions when you get behind the wheel."

"I've already heard *all* this from my dad."

"That's good advice in general. Try not to let emotions rule your decisions. Logic matters too. It's a balance."

"You should take your own advice," Hunter said, turning into the parking lot for customers. "You're dating my mom because you like her, but maybe you should think it over. Don't let those emotions make the decision."

One point for Hunter. He'd thrown it back in Hud's face. No one had ever said the kid was slow on the uptake.

"I *have* thought it over," Hud said, catching the keys when Hunter tossed them to him. "The girl I just told you about? That was your mom."

One point for Hud and the save.

Hunter stared at him blankly. "For real?"

Okay, well, Hud hadn't planned on it just coming out like that. He'd never had occasion to talk to Hunter about his history with Jo because why would he? It was all in the past, and while he would have loved it to stay where it belonged, they were still dealing with the repercussions. And it was time for Hunter to understand that this whole idea of being with Jo wasn't something he'd thought up on the spot at the last minute.

He met his gaze and didn't break eye contact. "For real."

Hud rolled back the shell of his truck cab and pulled out his equipment. The camp offered everything one would need to climb for rent, but years ago Hud had bought all his own stuff. He shoved a bag filled with harnesses into Hunter's arms.

He was still staring. "You and my mom."

"It was years ago. And we were both too young."

"But I thought you guys were just good friends. My friends said you had the hots for my mom, and I said no *way*, he's like my uncle." He scoffed. "You made me look stupid."

"It's complicated."

"I hate complicated."

Join the club, kid. Join the club. Come to the meetings. Pay your dues.

"Now I know why you don't like my dad."

The words hit Hud square in the solar plexus and he hadn't expected that. "Matt's a good man."

"But he took your girl."

"No, it's not like that. She's not property so she

can't be taken. And she had every right to go out with your dad. We weren't together at the time."

"But you wanted to be."

Hud grunted. "Yeah."

They hiked up to the entrance and checked in with Julian, one of the guides. With both an annual membership and employee discount, Hud could bring along a friend anytime, free of charge. Farther in, and at the craggy rock that sat at the base of Wildfire Ridge and faced away from the lake, Hud pulled out harnesses, helmets and ropes. He handed Hunter an extra pair of footwear because he was prepared.

Hud set them up, attaching the carabiner clip to the harness Hunter would use.

Hunter had been rock climbing here before, at least once on Friends and Family Day with Matt and his friends. So Hud knew he wasn't dealing with a complete beginner, but this would be the first time with him. And contrary to Matt, Hud had participated in extreme sports. He'd climbed El Capitan in Yosemite and other challenging boulders. But this wasn't a contest, Hud reminded himself, even if Hunter had called it.

He'd always been a little sensitive about Matt.

For the next hour, he and Hunter were locked in the symbiotic relationship between climber and belayer. Fearless, Hunter climbed, taking direction from Hud, always letting his feet lead him. Too many beginners used their hands to pull themselves up and wound up getting tired easily. Hunter was a quick study and when he was ready to switch places and be the belayer, Hud did his thing. The quiet between them wasn't awkward, but a comfortable silence.

The sun was beginning to set when Hud drove them back to Matt's house.

"I guess we won't be doing stuff like this any-more," Hunter said.

"Why not?"

"Think about it. You took me fishing and camping whenever Mom was off seeing one of Chuck's away baseball games. Before that, it was always whenever she went away for a trade show. But now, *you're* going to be the guy."

Holy crap. Hud had not seen that one coming. His chest constricted with the love he had for this kid. There was just no other word for it.

"I'm always going to have time for you, buddy."

Hunter snorted. "Grown-ups always say that. But…you still love my mom? For *real*?"

Hud didn't hesitate. "Yeah. I do. I never stopped."

"Wow, that's *hella* corny."

"Thanks."

"You should be *sure*, because you shouldn't fool around with a single mom."

"Preaching to the choir."

"Huh. Well, it's okay for you to date my mom, I guess. She should be happy. You better not be a jerk-off like Chuck or I'll have to kill you."

"Give me *some* credit."

"I'm serious."

"I am, too."

Hud parked on the sidewalk in front of Matt and Sarah's home. The light was on inside and he got to witness another domestic scene. Matt and Sarah in the window, as he wrapped his arms around her, pulling her in. There were an awful lot of new couples in Hunter's life. It had to be tough.

"They're so embarrassing to be around. Geesh." He climbed out of the car. "Whatever you do, don't get cutesy. It you call my mom honeybuns or sweetie pie, I swear I'll throw up all over you."

Hud smirked. "You got it."

They fist-bumped, and as Hud drove home, he thought this was about as good as life could ever get.

Chapter Sixteen

Joanne paced the living room, waiting for Hud. She'd never paced in her life, but that afternoon Hud had taken her son rock climbing on Wildfire Ridge. Hunter went up there a lot, whether with Matt or tagging along with Hud here and there, but this was the first time they'd been together since… Well, since Joanne and Hud became involved.

Considering Hunter wasn't thrilled with the idea of the two of them, Joanne had cause to be worried. Okay, so she had to stop freaking out. And when she heard Hud's truck pull up outside, she finally did. She ran to her window to see that at least from the outside, he was intact, no worse for the wear of hanging out with a sometimes-pissy teenager.

"You made it!" She threw open the door.

"What? You had doubts?" He rushed her at the door, picking her up and carrying her inside. "I've been through fires and pulled people out of wrecks. I think I can handle a teenager."

"And don't forget crawled under Mrs. Diaz's house for Pooky."

"What can I say? You fell in love with a real-life hero." He smirked as he put her down. "Who just got the green light."

"Oh my gosh, so he's okay with us dating?" She covered her mouth.

"Yep. But I *did* have to promise him a sports car on his seventeenth birthday."

Joanne gasped. "You didn't!"

"No, it's good. I'll take out a loan." He plopped down on the couch and stretched his arms to the side. "Don't worry, I should be done paying it off by the time I retire."

Poor Hud! She should have warned him, prepared him better. He had so much to learn about kids. They shouldn't be bribed, no matter how much you wanted to. The temptations came early. You couldn't do it, no matter how much you wanted to promise a gallon of ice cream, or a million dollars even, if they would just sleep through the night or let you go to the bathroom alone for once.

Then she caught the mischievous gleam in Hud's gaze. "You brat!"

He pulled her down on his lap, laughing. "Baby, if I'm going to mortgage our future over a sports car, it will be mine. Took you long enough."

Our future. She swallowed, her heart full. "You had me going."

His low throaty laugh was terribly sexy when it sounded like it came from a place of such deep contentment. She'd never imagined he would be this happy, dropped into her dull life. She had a mortgage payment and a 529 Education Fund for Hunter. She lived with a teenager and owned a plain Jane sedan good on gas mileage.

"I think now that we're officially together, you can stop all of the teasing." Her fingers grazed over his chin and the light bristle there.

"Hell, no. I was going to ramp it up." His arms came around her waist, and he slid her a slow smile.

That smile promised her a future and she would grab on and hold tight. This was everything she'd ever wanted. She framed his face. "Are you happy, Hud?"

"Why? If I say I'm not, are you going to do something to *get* me happy?"

He was incorrigible. Still, she giggled. "I might."

"Happier than I've ever been."

She waited, expecting him to tack on a teasing comment, like he'd be even happier if she brought him a cold beer. But he didn't make a joke. Hud knew when to be serious and that truth slid into her heart, warm and sweet. She tugged him up from the couch and he came willingly, smiling when he saw her turn toward the bedroom. They each took off their clothes and fell into bed, where he made love to her, slow and delicious.

Afterward, he crushed her against his chest. "I love you. I always have. And don't you ever forget it."

She kissed him and fell asleep with those words on her mind.

It took two more days and late-night talks with Hud, but Joanne made the decision about her new design.

"Where are you off to today?" Hud asked in the morning.

"The fabric store, lunch with my mother and Iris—" She bustled about the kitchen, pouring them each cups of coffee.

"Uh-oh. Does your mother know?"

"About us? Yes, she knows. And she's fine with it."

He held up his coffee mug in a mock salute. "I will accept that lie."

"Hud, you know she adores you," she chided, hugging his neck. "Stop."

"It's okay, baby. She adores me as your best friend, but I broke your heart once and I get that's hard to get past with your only daughter. I'm going to earn her respect back." He bent to kiss her on the lips.

"And what are you doing today?"

"Brought my toolbox and I'm going to fix your leaky sink. This is real hero stuff."

"That's why I love you." She finished her coffee, kissed him again and headed for the door. "I'll be back late because I have after-hours appointments with two different brides."

She'd gone ahead and scheduled an appointment with Brenda Taylor, with the explanation that she understood someone else would make the dress, but she wanted to talk about the designs she'd already bought. She left out talk of the new design, because in the end it might not be something Brenda would want anyway. Still, the meeting itself would go a long way toward clarifying that Joanne was no longer the jilted bride of the bad luck boutique. Someone was bound to see her coming inside the boutique. And as the influential Taylors of Fortune, their opinion would go a long way to getting the word out.

Joanne wore her yellow dress again. The bags were gone from under her eyes because these days she might be losing sleep here and there, but it was for all the right reasons. She was actually well rested, her skin clear and her cheeks rosy pink. And for the first time in a long while, she was happy in that over-the-top way that she figured was reserved for people younger than her.

Brenda showed up at the boutique a few minutes late. "Sorry, there was bad traffic. I had a deposition in Oakland today."

"We could have rescheduled." Joanne led her to the couch where her new design sat in the sketch pad, still not transferred to a graphic design program.

"Absolutely not. I'm really sorry with the way everything happened."

"You're not the first superstitious bride I've met, so don't be too hard on yourself."

"I'm not the superstitious one," Brenda said, settling back into the sofa. "It's my *mother*. Um, do you have some of that champagne around?"

"Of course." In the minifridge, Joanne found the uncorked bottle they hadn't finished when Jill had come in. Noting it still had fizz, she poured some into a flute and handed it to Brenda.

"Thanks. You're a class act. My mom expected you to get really mad and tell everyone in Fortune that we were taking our business elsewhere. And I wouldn't blame you if you did. My mother can be a real hypocrite."

"I'm okay with all that. That's not why I called you."

"Right. You said it was about the designs?"

"I didn't give you my best work. I like to hear the love story between a couple first. Whether they've always been secretly in love, or just discovered each other. Whether it's been on and off for years, or whether suddenly something just clicked. I didn't dig deep enough with you and I'm sorry."

"That's all right. I'm not the most romantic bride."

"Sometimes the dress tells the love story, but other times it's all about the bride. *Her* story." Joanne brought out her design. "What do you think?"

There was no mistaking the shock and longing in Brenda's eyes. Her fingers swept over the dress, as if it was already made. "This is amazing. It's just what I wanted but—"

"Couldn't put into words?"

"Exactly." She blew out a breath. "Or even had the time to find the words."

"That was my job, and I feel like I'm a little late in delivering. But I didn't make this design because I wanted to beg for the job back. It just came to me, and I want you to have it. Free of charge. No hard feelings."

"No," Brenda protested, finally looking up from the sketch. "That won't work. You have a lot of wedding expenses that bast—guy left you with. You were supposed to make the dress, too, which would have been more money for you."

"Don't worry. He's already paid me back in full. And do I *look* like I'm suffering?" She held out her arms to her side.

Brenda finally appraised Joanne, from the tips of her matching yellow flats to the collar of her dress.

"You look great. I guess being a jilted bride agrees with you?"

The confusion in her gaze was palpable. Joanne held back a laugh. "Sometimes things happen to us, and sometimes they happen for us. Other times we make things happen. And I'm happier than I've ever been."

"That's really good to hear. We don't all need to give into the patriarchy and get married. If you're okay, then no one else should care how you got there." She stood. "I want this dress, but I have to pay you for the design. I also want you to sew it for me. I'm not afraid of you touching my dress, or any ridiculous superstitions. I can see right now you're not despondent and incapable of focusing on sewing the dress. I trust you. I'm pulling rank on my mom. This is *my* wedding, after all."

Impressed that she'd been right and Brenda loved the design, Joanne stood. "Just sewing it for you will go a long way to repairing my boutique's image. I still don't want you to pay me for the design, but I do have an idea if you're interested."

A few minutes later, Brenda had gone, and Joanne had secured the first part of her plan. The doorbell chimed, and this time it was her next appointment. Leah, fresh-faced and so young. Joanne envied her in some ways. Leah would marry her first love, and hopefully she had a lifetime of happiness ahead of her. In a perfect world.

"I can't wait to see my dress design."

Joanne had so many ideas for Leah that she hadn't wanted to pare them down to one. The creativity was flowing out of her as if the well had been unplugged. Released. Leah was young, but she deserved choices. And if Joanne could give them to her, she would. Good thing she'd figured out a way to do that, with Brenda's help. She'd agreed to Joanne's plan. Brenda would pay for Leah's extra designs and help out with the differential on the expensive blue material that Joanne had located… In Paris, France.

"Good news," Joanne said as she pulled out the five designs she'd created for Leah. Each one was more romantic that the next. Flowing skirts, long trains, lace and satin.

So many choices, so little time.

"I moved a few things around and was able to put you into our bigger budget plan, so I have five different designs for you."

She gaped. "I thought I couldn't afford that."

Unwilling to make Leah sound like a charity case, Joanne fudged a little. "Well, I'm having a sale."

"Oh wow! That's great." Leah took a seat, accepting the white lie.

"And I found the perfect material for your blue dress. I hope you don't mind but depending on which design you choose, you might look a little like a certain older sister from the Frozen movie." She held up air quotes.

"That's what I was going for."

Joanne sat with Leah and together they went through the designs one after the other.

Chapter Seventeen

Hud wound up running to the hardware store three times. Once to get the part he needed, the second time to return the wrong part he'd been sold and the third time to return a defective one. This was plumbing. Suddenly a simple household fix meant his entire afternoon was gone. Well, plus letting Rachel outside every time she saw a bird through the sliding glass door daring to encroach on her new territory. She'd laid claim to Jo's house as her own before he had.

When his phone buzzed in his pocket, Hud fully expected to see a text from Jo, asking about dinner. Instead, he noticed he'd somehow missed a call from the station. He slid out from under the sink, bumped his head, cursed, and dialed back.

Ty picked up the phone. "We need you here ASAP. Wildfire Ridge is burning."

Hud wasted no time. He broke speed limits getting to the station. They needed all hands on deck before the winds allowed this wildfire to rage out of control. At the station, Hud suited up, knowing he had zero time to call Jo. She understood that because of his profession, from time to time he'd get called up. But he'd bet she never imagined it would be to Wildfire Ridge. It had been many years since there'd been so much as a brush fire up there.

"When did we get the call?" Hud asked Ty, as they rode in the engine truck together.

"A few minutes ago," Ty said. "One of the guides saw flames on the summit of the ridge. We've got Cal Fire units on standby from all over the Bay Area. We'll get this under control."

"We have to. There are people up there."

A few years ago, Wildfire Ridge had been hundreds of acres of open and protected land, but now there were guides that lived in trailers who worked for Wildfire Ridge Outdoor Adventures. Not to mention Jill and Sam, who had built their dream home on leased land. He wanted to believe they could keep the fire from reaching their property. But the important thing was limiting the loss of life. Both his men and those on the ridge.

When they arrived, they got to work immediately setting up a perimeter. Fire trucks pulled in and hoses were pulled out. The flames in the distance licked and rose from the trees like arrows, sending plumes of gray smoke in the sky. Hud quickly assessed just by the wind shift that the fire was moving fast. By tonight, if they didn't control this quickly, the entire hill would be taken.

Hud noticed when Alex kissed the cross on the chain he kept around his neck, like he did before they went into any burning building. Hud didn't have a ritual. His practice was to notice every single thing around him. The wind. Heat. Ground cover. To prepare for anything. This time, they weren't entering a contained structure. They were in open land where fire could move and jump practically unimpeded. Where, in fact, it was assisted by wind and dry tinder and brush. But they'd had controlled burns on the ridge which should have held. Still, the last time he'd been up on the property he'd noticed sagebrush too close to a trailer which needed to be cleared. He'd spoken to a guide about it. One could never be too careful.

Now this.

He moved closer to the fire, the flames making their own eerie crackling sound. The crew immediately moved to post up to the defensible areas: the house, the trailers where the some of the guides lived.

"Is J.P. here?" Hud asked.

"Either here or on his way," Ty said.

"He's not ready for this."

Hud found Sam outside with his hose, defending the home.

Jesus, Mary and Joseph. Save him from these can-do Marines that believed on some level they were invincible. "Sam, I don't advise this. Let us do our job."

"I could use your help," Sam yelled. "Not sending you away."

"You see those flames over there?" Hud pointed in the distance. "That could come up on us in minutes."

"Sam!" Jill screamed from behind them, climbing off an ATV. She'd apparently been on the other side of the ridge when she saw the flames.

"Get out of here, Jill! And take Fubar with you." He opened a gate, and out came their three-legged retriever, running toward Jill.

She picked him up and turned to her fiancé. "Samuel Hawker, I'm not going anywhere without you!"

"I just finished building this house!" he yelled back.

"We'll do everything we can do save it." Hud clapped him on the shoulder. "The good news is you listened, and you have plenty of defensible space between your house and any vegetation. That gives us time. Go with Jill. She needs you and we've got this."

That seemed to reach him a little, and then he caught Jill's eyes. "Please, Sam."

"Listen to her, man."

"Please."

With that last word from his lover, Sam folded. He dropped the hose and walked toward Jill, tugging her into his arms.

The crew advanced and sprayed the gel pretreatment on the house to keep the wood siding from getting hot as quickly. But it was certainly not a complete deterrent to the fire that kept moving. It would consume several acres per hour until they managed to contain it. As the wind shifted again, they kept the hoses aimed on the fire as it got closer, a sort of useless exercise when it came to this beast. He'd never seen this kind of fire behavior before. Both the intensity and speed were alarming.

Cal Fire crews from the Bay Area pulled in and went to work.

Two hours later, the fire had spread. It moved quickly, devouring everything in its path. Trees snapped. Bushes sizzled. The sky grew cloudy, gunmetal gray and ominous. As the sun slipped down the ridge, orange flames created their own kind of light. Beautiful and deadly.

"Where's J.P.?" Hud asked.

"He's here," Alex said. "Had the hose a minute ago but the chief sent him to help defend the trailer, the one closest to the vegetation. He's got another man with him. All the guides and residents have been evacuated."

"Not much of a defensible area there."

Suddenly an explosion lit up the night sky. Hud saw a trailer consumed in flames. No. Not J.P. He was too young. Too inexperienced. Hud ran toward the blaze, taking the hose with him. Two firefighters lay on the ground, obviously having been thrown. Flames were coming off one of them. Hud tackled him, rolling him until the flames were put out.

But it was only when he saw the Probation emblem on his helmet that Hud realized it was J.P.

As she locked up the shop and headed home, Joanne heard the sirens and, as was her habit, immediately thought of Hunter.

He's fine. A siren does not always mean an accident. It certainly doesn't mean it's Hunter who's been hurt. I have to stop being so paranoid.

Still, she checked in with him via text, making up an inane excuse, asking whether or not he was due to come home next week on Monday or Tuesday after school. She knew very well it was Monday but how else would she get him to respond? He was probably playing some video game when he should be doing his homework.

Hunter: D-uh. Monday.

Whew. Next, she thought of Hud, as had also become her habit, but he wasn't on rotation today, so she wasn't too worried. Joanne headed to the super-market, where she picked up ingredients to make dinner tonight. Usually he cooked, and while he was good at it and didn't mind, she was starting to feel like a slacker in that department.

She texted him:

I'm making Chicken Florentine tonight.

She smiled and added a heart emoticon just for kicks. It wasn't until she was in the checkout line along with other customers that she saw fire trucks careening down Monterey Street, one after another, sirens blazing. They weren't Fortune Valley Fire Department trucks. She caught San Jose and... San Francisco?

Dear God.

She pulled out her phone and texted Hud again.

Hey, what's going on? Are you home?

No answer.

A customer talking to the checker said, "I heard there's a wildfire on the ridge."

"What?" Jo interrupted. "Are you *sure* about that?"

"All you have to do is walk outside and you'll see the plume coming off the ridge. Plus, that's an awful lot of fire engines we just saw."

But that didn't mean a wildfire. It could be misinformation, she told herself. Hud had told her a million times not to jump to conclusions. Rumors spread like wildfire in their small town, way more than actual wildfires did. She knew this, and yet her heart wouldn't stop trying to beat out of her chest because Hud still hadn't replied. One text with no reply was no big deal, but two? He never ignored her like this.

She drove home, ignoring the rapidly graying and smoky skies, praying, envisioning Hud's truck parked in her driveway. It wasn't there. She rushed inside, forgetting the groceries. Tools were left on the floor near the sink, which Hud would never do unless he had to leave quickly. Rachel was outside in the yard and the minute she caught sight of Joanne through the patio door she began barking like a fiend to be let in.

Joanne did so, picking up the sweet dog and cuddling her. "Who's a good girl? You're spoiled rotten, you know that? I thought dogs were supposed to love outside."

This was Hud's fault. From the beginning, he'd treated Rachel like a little princess. Even the name he'd given her. He'd coddled her and given her treats and people food when she begged. Once, he'd cooked boiled chicken and rice, because he'd heard it was good for dogs. Let her sleep on the floor in his bedroom instead of in her perfectly good kennel.

That was because, despite the fact that Hudson

Decker was as big and rugged a man as any, he had the most tender heart she'd ever known.

The tears slipped down her cheeks then and she simply held Rachel on her lap, not knowing what to do. He still hadn't responded, and he wouldn't if he were on the ridge fighting a blaze. She was helpless again just when she'd finally taken control of her life. Just when she'd finally realized how much she loved him. It wasn't fair.

When the room finally darkened to the point where she should turn on a light, Joanne continued to sit in the darkness. Rachel eventually hopped off her lap and turned in circles, knowing something was wrong. Maybe smelling it in the air.

Then someone was tapping at the front door and Joanne rushed to open it, realizing she'd left it open. The thick air outside gave the night a hazy film. Joanne nearly choked on the stench of smoke. Zoey Davis, the Sheriff's new wife who owned the pet supply store in town, stood just outside the door. For a moment, Joanne didn't know what to think.

"Ryan asked me if I'd come and get you," Zoey said tentatively. "He thought you'd be scared if he sent one of his deputies."

Oh. God. Maybe if she hadn't said *that*. "Why? What's wrong? Is it Hud?"

"We don't know for sure," Zoey said gently. "But

there was an explosion, caused by one of the trailers on the ridge, and two firefighters were badly injured and taken by ambulance. Hud might be one of them."

Chapter Eighteen

Joanne didn't say a word during the drive to the hospital. Hard to talk, when she wasn't entirely sure that she could breathe. Rachel sat on Joanne's lap, because Zoey said she'd watch her when Joanne was inside the hospital. Joanne hadn't wanted to leave her behind, because Rachel *knew*. She knew something was terribly wrong. And right now, they needed each other. They both loved the same man beyond all reason.

This isn't happening. I've been afraid of all the wrongs things. Financial instability. Winding up alone. Reckless and careless driving. What I should have been afraid of all along was Hud's profession.

When he'd applied for the Fire Department, she'd actually researched firefighter deaths and found that around 45 percent of them were caused by heart attacks. That was nearly half, so she hadn't worried too much. He ate healthy—she helped with that—and was active. She'd been fooled, lulled into a false sense of security, because Hud was so good at his job. He'd never get hurt or killed. He took precautions. Mitigated the risks they all took and was compulsive about safety on the job.

And now he loved her and would never leave her again.

I above all people know that it doesn't work that way.

Fathers died suddenly and unexpectedly. Even when they had a family they adored and even when they tried to stay healthy. Sometimes it was DNA. Family history. The cruel twist of fate. Because of her father, Joanne's mother had become a widow. A single mother. And then Joanne had been a single mother.

Something she vowed never to be again. Yet she loved Hudson Decker with all her heart.

She thought she'd changed, grown, but she still had one major character flaw. The fault of a romantic. She still saw only what she wanted to see. With Chuck, she'd wanted to see a dependable man that she could eventually grow to love. Even if she should have seen the clear signs that was *never* going to happen.

Now she desperately loved a man that she wanted to believe would never leave her. But there were different types of abandonment.

Zoey dropped Joanne at the Emergency Room entrance. "I'll park and stay with Rachel. Don't worry."

Worry? Worry? Was she joking? "I think I'm going to be sick."

Zoey squeezed Joanne's arm. "Ryan's in there somewhere, and he'll help you. He's really good at that."

These were some of the comforts of a small town. A police presence with a sheriff who was also a friend to many. Deputies who went beyond the call of duty. The sheriff's wife, who came to your house to give you news she thought you should have.

Joanne walked slowly on boneless legs, through the swinging doors of the emergency room. What was she going to ask the triage nurse? She wasn't Hud's wife. Not actual *family.* Was she going to have to call the "best friend" card here? A maniacal sound came out of her that was a cross between a giggle and a sob. She overheard someone, perhaps a reporter, say that the firefighter had been taken to the second floor and was being prepped for transfer to the burn unit in Oakland. Joanne moved faster then, running to the elevator and punching the button like her life depended on it. Hud would not leave this hospital without seeing her first. No matter what.

She stepped off the elevator and in the next moment, she saw him. He stood in the hallway wearing his turnout pants and boots, soot all over his handsome face. A small group surrounded him. Ryan Davis and some of the other deputies.

"Hud," she whispered.

Before tonight, Joanne thought she'd understood relief. Comfort. But this moment was different. This was joy and emotion wrapped up so tight in her soul that it wasn't going to be able to stay inside. He turned, and his gaze swept over her in both surprise and worry, his brow creased. In two steps, he was at her side, taking her into his arms.

He smelled like smoke and fire but thank God, by some small miracle, her Hud was alive. Breathing. Now she could breathe.

"Hud, Hud, Hud," she said over and over again, sobbing, every single fear for him slicing through her, cutting her to the quick. With it came a storm of tears she didn't know how she'd ever be able to rein in.

She was vaguely aware of being carried somewhere, and after being set down, noticed that they were in a private waiting room. Alone. A TV was set to the local news, and a reporter broadcasted that several Fortune Valley firefighters had been hurt and in critical condition. They reported the fire was now 90 percent contained after several hours and hundreds of acres lost.

"I'm okay, baby. Listen. I'm okay." Hud just kept saying the words, calmly, like he hoped she'd eventually hear him through her fog. He pulled her down in his lap and rubbed her back until her sobs slowed. "I'm not hurt. It was J.P., our probie. He's badly hurt."

"What h-happened?"

"One of the trailers on the ridge exploded. There may have been gas inside or some other type of accelerant that caught. J.P. was closest when the blast hit. I don't know much about his condition. They won't tell me because I'm not...family." Those last words were said with an edge, as though he disagreed.

"I h-heard someone downstairs say that he's being taken to the closest burn unit."

"Yeah," Hud said. "Airlifted there."

She framed his face. "I was afraid they were talking about you."

"There was a lot of confusion when it all went down. Remember I talked to you about misinformation? The chief sent me in the ambulance with the EMTs to assist. I had firsthand information on his injuries, because I...found him."

There was a note of pain and despair in Hud's voice that she'd never quite heard there before. He was hurting, too, because this man was his friend and Hud hadn't been able to save him from being terribly injured.

She buried her face in his warm neck. "I'm sure there wasn't anything you could do. You always do your best."

"And sometimes it's not good enough."

"No. Don't say that."

"It's true."

"Where's his family?"

"On their way."

Joanne was afraid to ask the next question, but she did anyway. "Do you…have to go back out there?"

He took her hand and rubbed the back of it, looking at the ground. "I might have to. I don't know yet."

When Hud was informed that J.P. had been transported to the burn unit, he finally felt able to leave the hospital. He needed a shower and some rest before he'd have to get back out there again tomorrow. Even if the fire was contained, and he believed now that it just might be, there would be more to be done. There was also some damage control to do at home. He didn't like bringing his work home with him, but this was inevitable. The look on Jo's face, like she'd seen a ghost, might stay with him for a while. She'd worried over him before, of course, but everything had changed. They both now stood to lose much more.

Never before having been in the position where a

woman mattered this much to him, he didn't know how to handle her meltdown. He'd simply comforted. Assured her. Held her while she cried. But though he was okay, J.P. wasn't, and if he realized how easily that might have been him, he could only imagine the thoughts running through Jo's head.

She'd already had enough loss and turmoil in her life. Hud didn't want to add to it, but he was never going to be the one to walk away from her again. It might be selfish, because, sure, she might be better off with an accountant or a lawyer. Theoretically that was true, but one plus one didn't equal two in this scenario. He figured that was how it worked when a man was crazy in love. He was illogical enough to believe that he'd keep himself alive because he loved her.

When he walked outside the hospital, Rachel was waiting for him too, leaping for joy to see him and licking the soot off his face. Zoey dropped them off at Jo's house. He carried Rachel and slung an arm around Jo.

She stopped suddenly in the driveway. "The groceries. I left them in the car."

He took care of that, then he picked up the tools he'd left all over the kitchen floor. Regret spiked through him. She'd walked into this scene, knowing him and realizing something had to be terribly wrong. It struck him that, had he been home instead, he wouldn't have left this evidence everywhere.

"I need a shower." He came up behind Jo and squeezed her shoulders.

"Okay," she said, not moving, not turning like she usually did to kiss him.

"Baby, this doesn't happen very often. J.P. was a rookie. Young and inexperienced." He bent and spoke soft words brushing the shell of her ear.

She seemed to accept that. "I see."

"You've already looked up the statistics of firefighters who die in the line of duty, and I think you know the odds are in my favor. Long as I keep eating plenty of fish." He turned her in his arms and tried a smile, but it fell flat when she didn't return it.

Hud headed for the shower where he soaped up and let the water pound on tired muscles, taking away some of the aches. He waited, but Jo didn't join him as he'd hoped. This was definitely out of character for her lately, when she took every opportunity to be with him.

He dried off and stepped out of the bathroom, wearing only a towel around his hips, and was encouraged when he found Jo sitting on the bed. Her bare legs dangled from the side. She'd changed into one of his tees, the Giants one. He'd bet, as usual, there was nothing underneath.

"Are you hungry? I just threw a bunch of food away because it might have been in the car too long. Can't risk it. But I was going to make Chicken Florentine tonight."

He came to her side. "I'm sorry."

"No, it's not your fault." She stood. "But if you want to eat, I'll find something. You must be so tired."

With a palm, he pushed her gently back down. "I was but I rallied after I saw you."

"You're lying." She pulled on his towel. "But I want to believe you."

He removed his towel with a smile, because apparently, he had something to prove. Then his T-shirt came off, and as he'd suspected, nothing was under it. Nothing but bare sweet smooth breasts, creamy skin and sexy curves. He made love to her, taking his time, exploring every inch of her soft warm body. Just when he'd believed he had memorized the landscape of her body, what she liked and what turned her on, he discovered something new. He sank his teeth into her earlobe and felt her muscles clench around him as she moaned and climaxed.

"Hud, oh, Hud. Baby, I love you," she said into his neck.

And that was all he needed. The rest they could work out.

A while later, Hud rolled over in bed and reached for Joanne. Her side of the bed was empty. Normally after a day like the one he'd had, he would be tossing and turning all night. But he found he never had nightmares sleeping next to Joanne.

He found her in the kitchen, back in his T-shirt, opening cabinet doors and then bending down to write on a slip of paper.

"What are you doing?" he asked groggily.

"I'm writing a grocery list. Hunter comes home Monday and I want to make sure I have everything he likes to eat in stock. Or, everything he will eat, anyway."

"Baby, it's three in the morning."

"Did I wake you? I'll try to be quiet. Go back to bed." She bent to scribble on the paper.

"Can't you do this in the morning?" He came up behind her and nuzzled her jaw.

"No, I *want* to do it now. Anyway, I couldn't sleep."

Great. He'd somehow transferred his nightmares to her. "You should have woken me up."

"Why? You need to rest in case you have to…to go back up there tomorrow." Her voice shook.

"If you're not coming back to bed with me, I'll help." He glanced at her list, picked up the pen and added corn nuts. Hunter loved those things.

"They're bad for his teeth." She crossed it off, then bit her lower lip. "I can't think of the cereal he likes that's good for him. He's been gone a month and I forgot? What's wrong with me?"

Nothing a little sleep won't cure.

He kept quiet, going through her cabinets, not

knowing what to look for, or what could be missing. But he didn't want to leave her.

She threw the pen down. "I can't do this."

"It might be easier in the morning."

But then she was crying, so he doubted she meant the list. His heart felt as though a thousand daggers had struck him at once. He took her into his arms. "Tell me."

"I love you. I don't want to lose you. Ever."

"You won't."

"Tell me the truth. Did what happen to J.P. have anything to do with his inexperience, or was it just bad luck? Being in the wrong place at the wrong time?"

He didn't want to answer the question, but she already knew. Jo was smart. Capable. She was simply waiting for him to confirm the truth so she could make her point. "Mostly...bad luck."

"I thought so. It could have been *you*, Hud."

He pressed his forehead to hers. "But it wasn't me."

"This time." She wrapped her arms around this waist. "It's one thing for *me* to lose you. But it's another for our children to lose their father. I will not raise a child without a father. And I won't do this alone again."

Shit, well, he hadn't seen that coming. He was both flattered and hurt. She was already picturing their family, with him missing. Gone.

"What are you saying?"

"I'm saying that I love you, but I don't know how to do this. I don't know how to live with this fear. I don't know if I can."

"Jo, this is my job. My calling." Frustrated, he squeezed her arms and made her face him. "What you're really saying is you don't love me enough. Isn't that what you're saying?"

"Don't love you *enough*? How much is enough? I have never loved anyone like I love you. I loved you through our break-up, your car accident, through my accidental pregnancy, and you insisting on going to war!"

She looked pissed, like he had no right to live his life the way he wanted to. Not the way she insisted. Safe, when there was no such thing. He'd made a lot of stupid choices in his life, but every one of them had led him to where he was right now.

"Want to know what's enough? I loved you *enough* to give you away at your wedding, because I thought that's what you wanted." He pulled away from her then, angry and crushed beyond words. "I should go."

He found some clothes, grabbed his turnout gear and boots and left without another word. She didn't try and stop him. He couldn't believe they were ending like this. He'd just proven to himself his own sad theory. If Jo couldn't love him enough, maybe no one could.

Some freaking wonderful day this had worked out to be. J.P. was injured and Hud had no idea how badly, or if he'd ever make a full recovery. He was young. Too young for this to happen to him. When he was outside Hud realized suddenly that he didn't have his truck, since he'd been taken by ambulance with J.P.

With nothing but early morning dark and smoky skies for company, Hud walked all the way home.

Chapter Nineteen

The next morning, Joanne woke with swollen eyes. Crying all night could do that to a woman. Hud hadn't come back. She'd fallen asleep with her phone in her hands, expecting a text all night. He didn't even have a way to get home. She'd waited for him to walk back inside once he realized, to talk some more, and... What? Promise he'd never get killed and leave her alone for the rest of her life? He couldn't make that promise and Hud would never lie to her. Promise he'd give up his job for her? She would *never* ask that of him.

He had a friend in the hospital seriously injured, had been through hell himself, and she'd chosen that night to tell him that she couldn't do this anymore. Oh God. *Hud*. She hated herself right now. She'd never *stopped* loving him, but simply taken all that love and tucked it away somewhere deep inside of her, punishing no one but herself. For years. Then she'd taken a huge risk. Told him how she felt. He'd confessed his love for her. Now she'd screwed it all up and not only missed her lover but her best friend. She'd have to call Nora and Eve to cry and bitch over her latest man disaster. Hud was her disaster, because it seemed she couldn't yet figure out how to behave in a grown-up relationship.

She got out of bed and went through her morning routine of shower, brushing teeth, putting on the outfit she'd laid out the night before. Routine. It was important. She'd have to keep busy. Maybe invite Nora and Eve over for dinner. Hunter would be home soon. She had so much to do.

Thankfully, with two dresses to make in the coming months, Joanne would be busy with work, too. Which was good, because she didn't want to feel anything. Numb was all she wanted. She was done with love, done with all this emotion and fear of loss that wrapped around her heart and squeezed tight.

Having given Nora the day off, Joanne opened up the boutique late morning and tried to keep busy until time for Leah's appointment to be measured. When she arrived, she chatted happily about the wedding venue she'd secured, and her excitement over seeing her fiancé in "a short" six months. Joanne didn't know how the young woman did it. She was terrified to love a firefighter, but loving a military man came with its own set of pressures and risks. Leah seemed immune to them.

Either that, or she was just moving forward. One foot in front of the other. Loving him anyway because what else could she do? You couldn't always choose who you loved.

Shame did everything but cloud Joanne's vision, and after Leah left, she started to close up the boutique. She'd go home and work in her sewing room, where if she burst into tears at any moment, there was no risk of being seen by anyone. But then the door to the shop opened and there stood her mother, holding two cups of coffee from The Drip.

She smiled. "It's back! I've got my pumpkin spice, and for you, a mocha latte."

Joanne burst into tears.

"What's wrong?" She set the cups down. "I'll go get you the pumpkin spice instead, but I thought you hated it."

Joanne nodded but couldn't catch her breath.

Mom rubbed her back. "Yes, I should go get you a pumpkin spice, or yes you hate it?"

Joanne shook her head and staggered over to the sofa, grabbing a box of tissues on the way. She plopped down, covering her face.

"No, I shouldn't get you a pumpkin spice, or—?"

"Hud," Joanne managed between sobs, pulling out a handful of tissues.

"Oh God, no! Don't tell me he's been hurt. Someone at The Drip this morning said a firefighter had been killed!" Ramona covered her mouth.

Why wasn't Joanne better at charades? It would come in handy right now. Instead of waving her arms around to indicate a heart being pierced and shattered into a million tiny pieces, Joanne managed to say, "N-no."

"Oh thank God!" Ramona seemed to fall more than sit on the sofa next to Joanne. "What's wrong, then? Oh no! Is it—"

To end twenty questions, the ridiculous version, Joanne held her palm up in the universal sign for Stop. Composing herself, she dabbed at her eyes. "I broke up with H-hud."

"Oh boy. Why? Did you catch him cheating on you?"

"No!" Joanne glared at her mother and clutched the box of tissues on her lap. "But thanks for that image."

"Well, what on earth could it be? You're obviously crazy about him."

"Did you ever think maybe he's not that crazy about me? Huh? Huh?"

"Actually, no. I never considered that. You were busy on your wedding day, but I got to watch Hud pace. Every time he looked at you it was with longing in his eyes."

"W-why didn't you say something?"

"On your wedding day?" She went hand to chest. "It was a little too late. Besides, it really was no different than the way he's mooned after you since you were both sixteen. I really thought you saw it, too. Just figured you were ignoring it."

"Maybe I did, for a long time. Until I couldn't. And now… I'm too afraid to lose him to even try. I'm such a coward."

Her mother reached into her big hobo bag. "I think I have a book on fear in here. It's my latest bedtime reading."

"Can't you just give me the CliffsNotes version when you're done reading?" Joanne sighed.

"Fine." Ramona crossed her arms. "But is this about your father?"

"Daddy? No," Joanne said. "It's more about you."

"Me?"

"When he died, it nearly destroyed you. You struggled as a single mom, and then I struggled as a single mom. And I refuse to do that again."

"Honey, it wasn't your father's choice to leave us, any more than it was Matt's fault that you wouldn't marry him."

"It would have been a disservice to marry him when I still loved Hud."

But it was true that Joanne had been given a

choice between being a single mother and married to a man she didn't love. She'd chosen to be alone.

"A firefighter did get hurt yesterday, but not killed. He was a friend of Hud's."

"Oh, I'm sorry."

"It could have *been* Hud. And I keep seeing that. After the fire, I keep thinking that I could lose him. It's one thing to lose the man I love but another for his children to lose him. And I want more children. Hunter at least will always have Matt."

"Excuse me, but have you been given access to a crystal ball that I'm not aware of? How do you know Hunter will always have Matt? No one is guaranteed tomorrow."

"That's true, but with a dangerous job like Hud's…"

"Matt is a *pilot*, honey."

"It's true what they say about flying. Safer than driving," Joanne argued.

"And your father was a software engineer. It doesn't get much safer than that. I'm just sorry that your strongest memory is the one of me falling apart. Maybe I did in the beginning, but it didn't take me long before I realized that I'd been given a gift. All the years I had with him. A beautiful daughter with his eyes. His smile. His honor and strength. I chose a man with great character, and I'm proud that I had a child with him. I think that's some pretty choice DNA. Frankly, the genes of a hero might not be so bad, either. Besides, just think how beautiful your children would be."

"I wish I were stronger. I wish I were more like my young bride, Leah. She's not afraid to love a man in a *war* zone."

"Honey, you *are* strong. Indomitable. You need to remember that. Having a child as a teenager could have ruined your life. But you finished school, went on to study more and always put Hunter first. Single mothers are some of the toughest and bravest people in the world. You're just forgetting that because he makes you feel vulnerable."

"I love him so much."

"Then don't cut off your nose to spite your face, sweetie. Just pull up your big girl panties and *let* yourself love him. Risk it. It's always worth it, no question."

As expected, Hunter came home on Monday after school. Joanne was ready for him, and the talk she'd put off for so long. Too long.

"Hey, Mom." Hunter threw his car keys willy-nilly and they landed somewhere on the couch.

He was driving himself to school now, using his father's old truck. Nothing she could do about that. Kids grew up. It started the minute they left the womb and could no longer be protected. Not completely. Sometimes they made bad choices like drugs or smoking. She'd been lucky with her son in that respect.

Other times kids made honorable choices like joining the military. And her job was to support Hunter's choices, not fear them.

"You're going to lose those keys in the couch."

"Huh?" Hunter crunched into a crisp apple he'd picked up from the fruit basket on the coffee table.

"Never mind." He'd learn the hard way, when he couldn't find his keys and was late to class.

She was going to have to let go.

"What's for dinner?" This he asked between crunches, and due to dumb luck and being biologically connected, she was able to decipher it. Somehow.

"I ordered us a pizza."

He cocked his head. "Really? Cool!"

"Once a week we're going to splurge and eat all of the calories."

"Yeah, right." He plopped down on the couch, doubt heavy in his words.

She sat beside him. "I mean it. We should have a little fun here and there. It won't kill us."

"Yeah? Hey, where's Hud?" He looked around the room. It was the first time in a month he'd come over and not seen Hud. No wonder he'd ask about him.

"He's…probably at work." She took a deep breath and wished she could read from her prepared statement. She'd written everything down on paper but she wasn't sure she could trust herself to deliver it well. "Can we talk?"

"About what?" His eyes narrowed.

"You and me. I'm sorry if I didn't seem to care what you thought about Chuck. I should have paid more attention to the fact that you didn't like him. Somehow I thought you wouldn't like anyone I decided to get serious about."

He lifted a shoulder. "I like Hud."

She briefly closed her eyes against the ache just hearing his name caused. "Yes. I should have dated Hud."

How she would ever fix things between them, she still didn't know. But she was working on a plan and had a list started.

"Why *didn't* you?"

"That's kind of complicated. Hud didn't want to settle down for years and that's what I wanted. We also have a difficult past."

"Yeah, I know. Hud told me."

"I should have been the one to tell you, and I'm sorry."

"That's okay." He continued to crunch on his apple.

"I think I was afraid he'd hurt me again. So, I chose the safe way. Pretending I didn't still love him, but I always have. I never stopped."

He made a face. "Geesh. It's getting real sappy in here."

Joanne laughed and patted his knee. "This is the most important part for you to hear. If you still want to be a Marine, I'll support you."

At this, he set down the apple. "For real?"

"I know you can join with or without my approval, but I want you to know that it's your decision. I realize that I can't protect you. Nor is that my job anymore. You're a man and I'm going to treat you that way." She cleared her throat. "Well, at least I'll try."

"Hey, thanks, Mom." Hunter threw an arm around her shoulder.

Joanne pulled her son in the rest of the way for a hug.

She'd probably wear out her knees in another year or so, because her son was going to be a Marine.

Two days later, the fire on Wildfire Ridge had been contained. Only a small section of Sam and Jill's house had been destroyed and repairs would start soon. All the trailers were dust, however, but at least no others had exploded. No civilian had been injured. At a conservative estimate, hundreds of acres were taken. But the idea of destruction didn't really exist in nature. It would all come back given time.

Unlike buildings, some which were destroyed and never rebuilt. Rebuilding took more than the passage of time. It took hard work and money. Determination. Relationships, too, could die for a hundred different reasons, not the least of them being a man's pride. He hadn't spoken to or texted Jo in days and missed her like his right arm. Jo was his best and closest friend, and besides his parents, the only person who had loved him through careless and poor decisions.

What surprised him most was the anger he'd directed at himself. Anger and frustration that after promising himself he would fight to be with her, he'd walked out on their first serious argument. He should have turned around, gone back inside, and washed every fear away with logic. Made his case. But, tired of Jo finding reasons for them not to be together, he gave up. Which said a lot about his state of mind. Or maybe he was simply tired.

"Beer at the Silver Saddle?" Ty asked as they left the station.

"Nah, I'm not up for it."

He'd been a sad sack lately and was quite frankly getting sick of himself.

"Come on, man, I need a wingman tonight." Ty clasped his hands together, prayer-like.

"Not happening."

Ty gave up, hands tossed up. Good. Hud wouldn't need to make conversation with anyone tonight. He was in no mood for small talk.

He didn't need to be reminded that he'd had his first real date with Jo at the Silver Saddle. They'd started over that night. He'd made her wait, though that hadn't lasted long. Her pale blond hair had smelled like coconuts. She'd worn the short white dress he loved. His longing for her hadn't dissipated, and if it hadn't in ten years, he doubted it would in a few days.

What happens if I never get over her? The thought speared him; he didn't want to be alone for the rest of his life. He wanted children. A family. But he only wanted that with Jo.

He drove home, noting that in his quiet family neighborhood the Halloween decorations were already up. Lots of red, burnt orange and yellow. Pumpkins and gourds sat on porches and balconies. Witches and goblins were lawn decorations. The night was cold and crisp.

Mrs. Suarez sat in the rocking chair on her porch.

"Hey." Hud climbed out of his truck, shut the door and used the keyfob to lock it. "Everything okay with the thermostat?"

She sat with a serene smile curving her lips, nodding her head as she rocked. "Everything's fine, mijo. No te preocupa. Ella te amo. Mucho."

Hud nodded and wished once again that he'd had a passing grade in high school Spanish. All he got out of that sentence was "amo" meaning "love." He had to assume she loved the way her new thermostat was working. The magic of batteries.

"Yeah," he said, and went to unlock his front door, which was…already unlocked.

He cocked his head toward Mrs. Suarez, who was

the only one other than Jo who had a spare key to his home.

Mrs. Suarez covered her mouth and giggled.

Hud swung open the door, and that's when he saw her. She sat in the middle of the living room floor, Rachel on her lap. She'd created a picnic similar to the one he'd made for her the day she jumped in the lake after Rachel.

She wore the same short white dress he loved her in. Cowgirl boots with blue inlays. Her hair was down around her shoulders, loose and wild. She looked every bit like the beautiful girl he'd fallen for all those years ago but lost due to his own stupidity. And no matter how many gray hairs and wrinkles she would one day have, he would always see her that way.

"What's going on?" he asked.

"These are some of your favorite things." Her hand swept across the blanket.

There were two bottles of his favorite ale, a basket of oily looking French Fries from his favorite fast food place, and the king-sized cheesesteak sandwich that he loved.

She thought everything there was bad for his health.

"Does this mean…you're trying to kill me slowly?"

"No!" She laughed. "It means that you've always done so many nice gestures for me. The Bahamas re-creation. The picnic. And that's just a couple from over the years. You never forget my birthday. You never forget the anniversary that my father died. From now on, I want you to have everything you want."

"Everything I want?" He grinned.

"Moderation is the key." She stood and set Rachel down to the side.

"Hud, you have to understand. I'm a single mother and I've been stretched thin for years. I'm both strong and scared. Powerful and weak. But I recently discovered I don't really need a man in my life."

"Um, okay."

She fanned her hands. "This is coming out all wrong. What I meant to say is, I don't need a man in my life. Not just any man. I need you, Hud, because I love you. I don't love you because I *need* you. Am I making sense?"

"Yeah," he said, taking a step toward her. "Perfect sense."

"Oh, whew." She made a show of wiping at her brow. "I'm not very good at this."

"Eating crow is usually my job, so I'm going to cut you some slack." Closing the small distance between them, he took her hand, raised it to his lips.

"Actually, Jo, this goes both ways. I shouldn't have walked away that night. I said no one could or would scare me away, and then I let you do it. My mistake."

"I forgive you. Now would you please forgive me

and let me be your girlfriend again? I mean, I know that I'm a handful." She kept talking as if she had to make her case. "I can be neurotic and—"

That's when he shut down the rest of her words with a kiss. "You're all I've ever wanted."

Her eyes were shiny with unshed tears, but he knew enough to know these were the "good tears."

"You're a good man. I love that you were always such a good friend to me, I love how you help others, like Mrs. Suarez. And I love that you're a real life hero." She took a breath.

"Do you want to know how long it took me to get over you?" Her voice broke. "Never. I never got over you."

She'd had his heart long ago. Hud tugged her into his arms. Yeah, it was official. He was never going to let her go again.

Joanne gazed up at him, her green eyes shimmering. "I used to call you the fun in my life. But you're the *love* of my life, Hudson Decker, and I want to spend the rest of my life with you."

Relief flooded through him, knowing he now had everything he'd ever wanted right in his arms. He kissed the woman it seemed he'd always loved.

In his grasp he held both his past and his future rolled into one.

Epilogue

Eight months later

Joanne clutched Hud's hand as he drove them up the hill to Wildfire Ridge. It was the first time she'd been here since the wildfire, but it was for a very good reason. There would be a wedding here today.

A cause for celebration on the ridge.

"Man, it looks almost spooky up here," Hunter said from the back seat. "Bummer."

"Don't worry. It's all coming back," Hud said, and squeezed her hand.

In the distance, parts of the ridge were barren and battered. Desolate. Trees were missing or torn in half, black and charred. But here and there, nature was rallying. Sprigs of fresh green grass pushed through the damp earth. The early spring weather was mild after the blessedly long rainy season they'd desperately needed.

Thankfully, J.P. would make a full recovery. Only later had Joanne found out that Hud would receive a commendation. He'd pulled J.P. away from the blast at great risk to himself. After the initial sharp pull of shock and dismay that Hud would risk his own life to save another, Joanne had moved swiftly to pride in her fiancé. She continued to work hard every day at choosing love over fear. She'd been with Hud to see J.P. several times after the fire and he'd joked about how soon he could get back to work and kick everyone's butt at fireman's poker. Hud told him to take it easy and enjoy the rest because when he got back, he'd be working his ass off.

For now, weddings were in the air. Leah and her husband, David, had been married outside at Fortune Valley Family Ranch only a month ago. The dress had turned out beautifully, if Joanne said so herself. Both bride and groom were beautiful, young, and wearing matching blue. David, soldier rigid, holding his head high, proud to be marrying such a wonderful girl. She'd become very special to Joanne, too. They'd had long talks every time Leah had dropped by just to see how the dress was coming along. She'd started working part-time at The Drip and Joanne would see her there, too, every time she picked up a decaf soy latte.

And even though Joanne had once thought she'd be married outside too, she and Hud would be married in her mother's church. The same place her parents had married forty years ago. Hud's parents were coming out and it was going to be a big wedding. Big enough that they'd booked the hall in town to fit everyone at the reception. She was sewing her dress, too, this time. The "dream" dress. Everything seemed to take her a little longer these days, and even with Nora's help, the dress would take a few months, which was fine.

She wouldn't need it until after the baby was born.

Hud parked and came around the passenger side to open the door. He put down the stool they'd been using lately and offered Joanne his hand.

"Can you make it up the rest of the way?"

She hefted her rather large body out of the truck with Hud's assistance, stepping on the stool and then the solid ground. Good Lord, she was huge this time. Somehow unable to break with tradition, Joanne was again pregnant before marriage. It was a little embarrassing at her age, but on the other hand, good to know all parts were still present and accounted for. Still working. When she'd found out and done the math, she estimated that she'd become pregnant the night she and Hud had reconciled. In their hurry, they'd forgotten about protection. It only took once.

It was a happy surprise.

Hud was ecstatic, especially when the ultrasound had revealed a girl. He'd actually proposed to Joanne before she'd even missed her period. He'd dropped to a knee on a picnic blanket in the middle of his living room. They did love their traditions. He'd given up his house and all three of them were now living together in hers. Both he and Hunter were working on the baby's room, painting the walls pink and putting together the crib. Hunter had adjusted well, too, and was just as excited about the baby as they were. He'd been hoping for a brother, but he might still actually get one. Matt's wife, Sarah, was newly pregnant. Plus, of course, Joanne didn't think she wanted to stop at just one child with Hudson. She wanted at least one more.

Joanne lumbered up the hill toward the row of outdoor seats, Hud holding one arm, Hunter the other one. Between the two of them they nearly carried her up the hill.

"I'm good," she protested, but neither one of them gave up until she was safely seated in a chair.

Hunter went off to find a friend and Hud sat next to her, holding her hand. He carefully brushed a stray hair from her face, making her smile. Her best friend had turned out to be such a romantic. He claimed she brought it out of him, but he was so good at tender words and thoughtful gestures with her that it almost seemed like he'd been planning it all. Once she'd laughingly accused him of that, and he'd simply met her gaze, eyes deep and penetrating.

"For years."

Some days, she also regretted their wasted time. All the years they'd danced around each other but never taken the leap to be together. She might have been able to have five kids with Hud had they started early enough. When she'd told him this, he'd staged a mock heart attack, clutching his chest.

"Five kids? I'd have to work until I'm seventy."

Sure, the pregnancy hormones had made her a little emotional at times, but she was happier than she'd ever been. Determined to look forward and rarely into the past unless absolutely necessary.

The music began to play, and Jill's bridesmaids filed out, one after the other. Among them Zoey Castillo-Davis and Carly Cooper, her two best friends. Joanne had had to alter Zoey's dress when she also learned she would be five months pregnant at the time of the wedding. She walked up the aisle arm in arm with her husband, Sheriff Davis. Carly followed, holding the arm of her husband, Levi. Two more bridesmaids were arm in arm with the guides, Julian and Michael.

Heartfelt vows were exchanged, both Jill and Sam near tears. Joanne reached for the now ever-present tissues in her purse and dabbed at her eyes. Out of the corner of his eye, Hud smiled, winked and squeezed her hand. She knew what he was thinking. That would be the two of them soon enough. Professing their love for each other in front of a crowd of on-lookers. Their baby girl watching from the sidelines. She couldn't wait.

It was a beautiful wedding, Jill and Sam's spacious house on the hill as a backdrop. It stood as a reminder of how close they'd come to losing it all. But they'd rebuilt the structures, and let time and nature heal the rest. Wildfire Ridge would soon bounce back with renewed growth. Wildflowers would bloom again. Trees would grow tall.

And Joanne would be here to witness it all coming back, right next to her handsome firefighter hero.

* * * * *

WE HOPE YOU ENJOYED
THIS BOOK FROM

HARLEQUIN
SPECIAL
EDITION

Believe in love. Overcome obstacles. Find happiness.

Relate to finding comfort and strength in the
support of loved ones and enjoy the journey
no matter what life throws your way.

6 NEW BOOKS AVAILABLE EVERY MONTH!

Daisy went over to the bassinet and lifted out Tony,
cradling him against her. "Of course. There's lots
more video, but another time. The footage of what the
ranch looked like before Noah started rebuilding to the
day I helped put up the grand reopening banner—it's
amazing."

Harrison wasn't sure he wanted to see any of that. No,
he knew he didn't. This was all too much. "Well, I'll be
in touch about that tour."

*That's it. Keep it nice and impersonal. "Be in touch"
was a sure distance maker.*

She eyed him and lifted her chin. "Oh—I almost
forgot! I have a favor to ask, Harrison."

Gulp. How was he supposed to emotionally distance
himself by doing her a favor?

She smiled that dazzling smile. The one that drew him like nothing else could. "If you're not busy around five o'clock or so, I'd love your help in putting together the rocking cradle my brother Rex ordered for Tony. It arrived yesterday, and I tried to put it together, but it has directions a mile long that I can't make heads or tails of. Don't tell my brother Axel I said this—he's a wizard at GPS, maps and terrain—but give him instructions and he holds the paper upside down."

Ah. This was almost a relief. He'd put together the cradle alone. No chitchat. No old family movies. Just him, a set of instructions and five thousand various pieces of cradle. "I'm actually pretty handy. Sure, I can help you."

"Perfect," she said. "See you at fiveish."

A few minutes later, as he stood on the porch watching her walk back up the path, he had a feeling he was at a serious disadvantage in this deal.

Because the farther away she got, the more he wanted to chase after her and just keep talking. Which sent off serious warning bells. That Harrison might actually more than just like Daisy Dawson already—and it was only day one of the deal.

Don't miss
Wyoming Special Delivery *by Melissa Senate,*
available April 2020 wherever
Harlequin Special Edition books and ebooks are sold.

Harlequin.com